P9-CMT-313

Also by Patrick F. McManus

The Bear in the Attic

The Deer on a Bicycle

Kid Camping from Aaaaiii! to Zip

Never Cry "Arp!"

Into the Twilight, Endlessly Grousing

How I Got This Way

The Good Samaritan Strikes Again

Real Ponies Don't Go Oink!

The Night the Bear Ate Goombaw

Whatchagot Stew

Rubber Legs and White Tail-Hairs

The Grasshopper Trap

Never Sniff a Gift Fish

They Shoot Canoes, Don't They

A Fine and Pleasant Misery

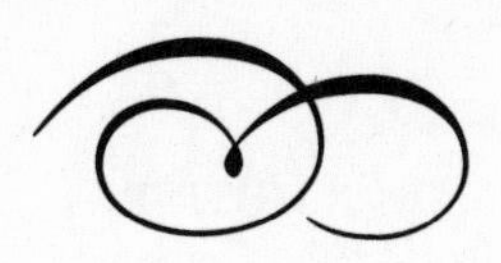

The Blight Way

A Sheriff Bo Tully Mystery

Patrick F. McManus

Simon & Schuster
New York London Toronto Sydney

SIMON & SCHUSTER
Rockefeller Center
1230 Avenue of the Americas
New York, NY 10020

For information about special discounts for bulk purchases, please contact Simon & Schuster Special Sales at 1-800-456-6798 or business@simonandschuster.com

Book design by Ellen R. Sasahara

Manufactured in the United States of America

2 3 4 5 6 7 8 9 10

Library of Congress Cataloging-in-Publication Data

McManus, Patrick F.
The Blight way / Patrick F. McManus.
p. cm.
1. Rocky Mountains—Fiction. 2. Outdoor life—Fiction.
I. Title.

PS3563.C38625B55 2006
813'.54—dc22
2005051637

ISBN-13: 978-0-7432-8047-1
ISBN-10: 0-7432-8047-4

To Darlene

The Blight Way

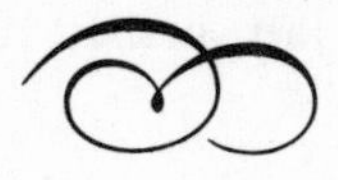

Chapter 1

After happily noting that the mud puddles of the parking lot had frozen over during the night, Blight County Sheriff Bo Tully momentarily regretted having established the departmental policy that neither he nor any of his deputies could use obscenities while on duty. Otherwise, he would have uttered a four-letter one at the sight of Jan Whittle. She was frowning at him from the back doorway of the courthouse, hands on hips. Tully decided that his stomping a few puddles on the way into the courthouse would not please Jan Whittle. Stomping frozen mud puddles was one of his great satisfactions.

He pulled his Explorer into the sheriff's reserved parking spot and got out. Jan rushed him the second his feet hit the ground.

"About time you showed up," she snapped. "I'm almost late for school."

She was principal of Delmore Blight Grade School.

Tall and thin, with rather sharp features, Jan seemed to be a person in a permanent rush.

"Sorry," he said. "If I'd known you were waiting for me, I'd have gotten here earlier."

"Oh, sure," she said. "Listen, I want you to go after that Cliff boy right now. He's been off in the Hoodoo Mountains for six weeks!" Jan had the annoying habit of focusing her entire attention on the person under interrogation, probably something she had learned in her years as a teacher.

"No way," Tully said. "I chased that brat all over two mountain ranges last year, and I'm not doing it again. Besides, it'll snow up there soon. He'll get sick of that quick enough."

"He'll get sick of that! Glen is only twelve years old!"

The boy, Glen Cliff, simply didn't like school. To his credit, he would try it for a couple weeks each September, see that he didn't like it any better than the year before, then take off for the mountains. Bo Tully hadn't been much different himself, as far as school was concerned.

"Listen, Jan, I'll see what I can do. I've got murders to solve and stuff like that, but if I get a break in my schedule, I'll go up and have a look for the kid, okay?"

"Murders to solve! Don't make me laugh!"

Jan Whittle didn't seem to be in much danger of laughing. She spun on her heel and stomped over to her car, smashing the ice on several puddles as she went. She needed to work on her technique some, Tully mused, no doubt about that.

Tully wondered if she remembered that when they

were both in sixth grade she had been his girlfriend for a while. It was possible, he supposed, that she hadn't realized she was his girlfriend, since they had never even talked. But that's how love affairs in sixth grade had been back then. Her dark brown hair had streaks of gray in it now, but she had aged nicely, keeping herself trim and fit. Too bad she was still married to Darrel Whittle, the oaf of a city attorney. Otherwise, he wouldn't mind dating her again. Maybe this time they would even talk.

Before entering the courthouse, Tully checked his image in the glass door. He turned to check his side profile. Perfect. Sticking to Atkins for two months had stripped twenty pounds off his six-foot-two frame. Feeling instantly energetic, he ran up the marble stairs that led to the main floor.

The Sheriff's Department occupied a large suite of rooms in the rear of the building, with the jail directly beneath. A hallway stretched the length of the building, with a couple dozen watercolors displayed on the walls. For once, Tully approved of the paintings. They were good. Clearly the artist was a person of considerable talent.

As he entered the office, he was amazed to see that both the night shift and day shift had managed to leave one medium-dry doughnut on the tray next to the stainless steel coffee pumps. Probably because it had been dropped on the floor. Tully took his Picasso clown mug off its hook and pumped the decaf. It sputtered and fizzed out half a clown's worth.

He sipped the lukewarm coffee and munched the doughnut as he strolled through the briefing room. Tully thought the walls had been painted puce. He didn't know what color puce was, but it had the right sound. His undersheriff, Herb Eliot, gave him a nod from the doorway of his own cubicle and went back to his newspaper. The Blight County Sheriff's Crime Scene Investigation Unit was hunched over his computer. Byron Proctor solved more crimes with his computer than did the rest of the department put together. Tully figured that hiring the kid had raised the average IQ of the department by at least ten points. Byron had short brown hair, most of which seemed engaged in an effort to stand straight up. He wore rimless glasses half an inch thick perched on an overly large nose. He had both the posture and complexion of a clam. He was twenty-seven years old and, as far as Tully was concerned, a genius. He had several visible tattoos. He might also have had body piercings, but Tully didn't want to hear about those.

"Hey, Lurch!" Tully yelled at him across the room.

Byron looked up from his computer and grinned his snaggletoothed grin. "Hey, Sheriff!"

Tully had given Byron his nickname, Lurch. He was the kid's hero.

At forty-two, Tully's thick brown hair was already going gray. So was his thick brown mustache. The mustache drooped crookedly over one corner of his mouth, possibly a result of his tugging on it whenever he had to do some hard thinking. His nose had been struck more than once with a hard object, fortunately so, in Tully's opinion, for otherwise he might have been far too good looking.

"Morning, Sheriff," Daisy Quinn said, perkily. With

short black hair and brown eyes, she was small and compact and gave off an aura of pure efficiency. She wore a white blouse beneath an open gray vest and a tiny black skirt. "Your mom called. Said to remind you again to get a haircut. She's tired of you going about 'practically looking like a hippy.' Her words."

"Yeah yeah," Tully said. He treated Daisy to a quick grin. He was pretty sure Daisy was in love with him. Then, what woman wouldn't be? Well, sure, Jan Whittle. Can't please everyone.

As he entered the door of his glassed-in office, he noticed that a fly had paused on the window behind his desk. It was a good fly. Not a great fly by any means but still a good one. Apparently engrossed in the view of Lake Blight, the fly failed to detect the sheriff's approach. Tully picked up the swatter from his desk, whopped the fly, flipped the swatter over and caught the tiny corpse in mid-fall.

"You are *so quick!*" Daisy said, watching him from her desk.

"Thanks," he said. He tipped the swatter and rolled the fly onto the windowsill. Aside from being dead, the fly was still in good shape. He gave the sill two sharp raps with the wire handle of the swatter. Then he stood his index finger up straight as a sentinel in front of the fly. Wallace scurried out from his lair behind the gray metal filing cabinet, stopping in front of Tully's finger. It could have gone around either side and grabbed the fly, but Wallace knew the rules. Trembling with eagerness, the spider waited, twitching ever so slightly forward, until the sheriff slowly raised his finger to a full stop.

Only then did Wallace rush in, grab the fly and haul it back behind the filing cabinet. Tully imagined Wallace smacking his lips. If he had lips. If he was a he. This was a fairly choice fly.

"I wish you'd stop fooling with that spider," Daisy said. "It gives me the creeps. One of these days it's going to nip your finger. It could kill you, Sheriff, if it's one of them Hobo things."

"Danger's my game," Tully said. "Besides, I like getting into a spider's mind. Gives me an edge on our clientele."

"Speaking of spiders," Daisy said. "If you have a moment for some law enforcement, Batim Scragg's on the phone. Says he's got to talk to you right away. Line one."

Batim Scragg. Tully had once put Batim in prison. Later he had done the same for Batim's two sons, Lem and Lister. He picked up the phone.

"Sheriff Bo Tully here. How you doing, Batim?"

"Doing fine, Bo. How you?"

"Fair to middling. To what do I owe the honor?"

"Well, I kinda got this situation out here at the ranch. Fust thing I got to tell you, though, me and the boys we ain't got nothing to do with it. Hey, we'd done it, there wouldn't be no awkward situation at all, you get my drift."

Tully tugged on the corner of his mustache. "I get your drift, Batim. So what is this situation?"

"We got a dead body draped over one of our pasture fences."

There was a pause at Tully's end.

Batim said, "Bo?"

"Yeah, go on, Batim, I was just thinking."

"I know what you was thinking. But if me or the boys had anything to do with it, there wouldn't be no body hanging over one of our fences. You know that. I wouldn't be on the phone discussing the matter with you neither."

"Exactly my thought, Batim. So what kind of body is it?"

"We ain't been near it. Course the boys wanted to go fool with it, but I said no, it might be a crime scene and the sheriff won't want you messin' round out there. That's what I told them, Bo."

"Good for you, Batim."

"But I did take a look with the binoculars and it appears to be a white male dressed in a dark-blue pin-stripe suit. Got a shiny black shoe on one foot and only a black sock on the other."

Crime scene. White male. Batim was up on his TV police jargon. Everyone in the whole country talked that way now.

"Pinstripe suit," Tully said. "Doesn't sound much like any of our local characters. Make sure nobody goes out there, and I'll get a deputy over to secure the scene. Buck Toole's up near Famine right now. Should be there in half an hour. I'll be up pretty quick myself. You tell the boys they better not mess with Buck, they know what's good for them."

"You got it, Bo."

Tully hung up. "Daisy, get in here and bring your pad!"

Daisy scooted in, lowered herself into a gray metal chair, her back straight, pencil poised.

"Okay, we apparently got a body draped over a fence out at the Scragg ranch. Batim certainly knows a dead body when he sees one. Get Florence to radio Buck Toole and tell him to get over to the Scragg ranch up past Famine. Pronto. Tell him to let us know right away what he finds out."

Herb Eliot had come over from his cubicle and leaned against the door frame, listening. "You letting Buck go onto the Scragg ranch all by himself? He's the dumbest guy we got. Which is saying something!"

Tully tugged on his mustache. "Herb, you of all people should know this, but there are times for dumb in law enforcement. This is one of them. You can't get just anybody to go on the Scragg ranch all by himself. Anyway, Daisy, you better alert that new medical examiner that we have some work for her. What's her name again?"

"Parker. Susan Parker. Came up from Boise yesterday. Very pretty."

"Really? How pretty?"

"About half as pretty as I am."

"All right then!"

Daisy laughed, obviously pleased.

"Next, get hold of the old man and tell him to throw together his camp kit. And a bunch of those smoked elk sausages he makes. We may be spending a few days roughing it."

Eliot said, "You taking Pap?"

"Yeah, it's the sorry old devil's seventy-fifth birthday. No present he'd like better than a good juicy murder.

But don't say anything about a body, Daisy. I want to surprise him. His birthday and all. Plus he knows the Scraggs inside and out."

"Geez, seventy-five," Daisy said. "He sure doesn't look it. Shoot, I'd date him myself."

"A lot of women have lived to regret those very words," Tully said. "Oh, and I don't want him armed. He shows up with a gun, he ain't going, you tell him that."

"You bet."

"One more thing. Call Bill Fetch at the State Police. Tell him we seem to have a dead body up at the Scragg ranch a couple miles north of Famine. Ask him to get one of his troopers up there soon as he can, to protect the scene. Be sure to tell him we got Buck on the way. Bill will understand the need for haste."

He got up and walked to the door of his office and yelled across at the Crime Scene Investigation Unit. "Lurch, I want you to stay in the office all day. I may need you up at Famine."

"I'll stick around all day, Sheriff. All night, too, if you need me."

Tully went back to his desk and finished off the doughnut as he replayed Batim's phone call in his head. This was probably the first time in his life Batim Scragg had cooperated with the law. Probably the first time any Scragg in the whole history of the world had cooperated with the law. But Batim didn't fool him for one second. If there was a murder, Tully would simply sort Scraggs until he found the culprit.

He unlocked his office gun safe and took out a Winchester .30-30 carbine, a 12-gauge Remington 1100 semiautomatic shotgun and a Glock 9 mm with belt holster. He loaded them and put extra shells for each in a leather gym bag, including a box of Number 8 bird shot.

Herb gave him a puzzled look. "Eights?"

"Yeah. Never know when you might run into a flock of quail either going or coming from the Scragg ranch. Got to work in your hunting where you find it. Number eights work pretty well for getting a Scragg's attention, too."

"I guess. Wouldn't tear one of them up terribly much, at least if he had enough sense to be running away."

As an afterthought, Tully added a Colt Woodsman .22 pistol that he sometimes liked to tuck in the back waistband of his pants, or even down one boot, just in case. He checked the clips of each pistol. Full. Before replacing the clips, he pulled back the slides to make sure the chambers were empty. People were all the time shooting themselves and others because they forgot to check the chambers on their auto pistols. He slipped the Colt into the pocket of his suede sports jacket.

One of the few perks of being sheriff was that Tully could dress pretty much any way he liked. Today he wore cowboy boots, jeans and the suede jacket over a tattersall shirt open at the collar. He wore his sheriff's uniform only when the county commissioners required the department to march in a parade, on which occasions he and his deputies looked like a strange assortment of disgruntled Gene Autrys who had lost their horses.

Tully didn't know who had come up with the design

for the uniform, but he suspected his own father, Eldon "Pap" Tully. Pap had always fancied himself something of a cowboy. Tully had worn the uniform for five years himself, before he replaced Pap as sheriff. Tullys had been sheriffs of Blight County for over a century, except for a couple of brief intervals when the voters had suffered a lapse of sanity.

The rifle hanging by its sling from his shoulder, the shotgun in one hand and the bag in the other, Tully walked out through the briefing room. Eliot had gone back to his newspaper. "Hold down the fort, Herb!" Tully yelled at him. "And don't do any thinking on your own, okay?"

Daisy stifled a giggle. Lurch did his snaggletoothed grin.

"Right, Sheriff!" Herb yelled back without looking up from his paper.

As Tully ambled over to his parking spot behind the courthouse, some of the current residents of the jail stopped shooting baskets long enough to give him their hard stares through the wire mesh of the exercise cage.

He held up the shotgun. "Expect some company, boys!"

Sorry nincompoops. Nobody ever told them you can't be dumb. Half of them wouldn't live to see thirty, done in by booze, drugs, cars, AIDS, guns, knives, pool cues, enemies and friends. Mostly friends. The inmates intensified their hard stares. The stares were meant to tell him that as soon as they got out they'd settle the score with him. Two former inmates had actually tried. They hadn't made it to thirty.

He climbed into the mud-coated, red Ford Explorer and clamped the shotgun upright in its clip on the dash. He slid the .30-30 into a gun rack attached to the heavy wire screen that separated the front seat from the back. The gun rack also contained a fly rod, separated into its two sections but rigged with leader and fly, a size fourteen Dave's Hopper. A man had to be ready. He locked both handguns in the glove compartment. As he drove out of the parking lot, he grinned at the inmates hanging against the wire. They didn't grin back.

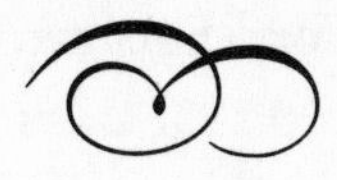

Chapter 2

Pap was sitting in a rocker on his covered front porch. He was medium height and lean with a thick shock of pure white hair protruding around the edges of his battered black Stetson. A classic wood-and-canvas pack frame was propped against a white porch column. An insulated cooler sat next to it.

Pap lived alone in the huge house that sat on a hill overlooking what Pap had once clearly thought of as his domain. Probably still did. Visitors to Blight County might wonder how a person earning a sheriff's salary for nearly forty years could afford such a fine house. The residents of the county, on the other hand, had no doubt.

Pap walked out to the Explorer and loaded his pack into the rear luggage area. He went back and got the cooler and put it inside the SUV. Then, grunting a bit too graphically to suit Tully, he hoisted himself up into the front seat.

"You practically need a ladder to get into this rig," he complained.

"You better not have a gun stashed in that pack," Tully said.

"Course I ain't. And what's the idea of you having that saucy little broad of yours tell me what I can bring and what I can't! What I need a gun for, anyway?"

"What difference has that ever made?"

Tully watched his father fuss with the seat belt.

"How you fasten this infernal thing?"

"Like this, for the thousandth time!" Tully reached over and snapped the belt latch shut. What was it with old people and seat belts? He'd never met an old person yet who could fasten one. Pap could tear apart a car and put it back together blindfolded but couldn't figure out how to fasten a seat belt.

"Happy seventy-fifth, Pap."

"Thanks. So what did you get me?"

"Same as every year. Nothing. Which is more than you deserve. Actually, I do have something."

"I probably won't like it."

"Oh, you'll like it all right. We apparently got ourselves a murder up by Famine. Batim Scragg called up this morning and said he had a body hanging over one of his fences."

"Awful thing," the old man said. "Murder." Beneath the stormy white brows, the hard little eyes sparkled with sudden delight. "Thanks, Bo. For taking me along. Been a while since I've had a good murder. Couldn't be more pleased if you'd bought me something."

"I figured you might like it."

"I hope it's an actual murder, not just a killing. It would be nice there was something for me to solve. I hate it when all you got to do is go down to the nearest bar and arrest the guy that's bragging about the killing."

"Hey, you're talking about my life," Tully said. He had to admit, though, that a real murder might be a nice change of pace.

He turned the Explorer out onto the highway and headed north toward Famine.

The valley stretched away on either side of the highway with the Blight River meandering a parallel course far off across mildly undulating grasslands. The river banks were lined with cottonwoods, their fall leaves now only tatters dancing in the wind. Tully thought of the leaves as Cadmium Yellow Light. Beyond the river, to the east, the Snowy Range of the Rockies surged up abruptly from the valley floor. To the west, the ragged granite peaks and ridges of the Hoodoo Range protruded above the banks of morning fog.

The old man pointed to a small patch of yellow high up on the evergreen slopes of the Hoodoos.

"Grove of aspen," he said. "Aspen mean there's water nearby. Don't mean the water's easy to get, though."

"You had a mine up near those aspens," Tully said. "You and Pinto Jack. Back in the fifties. One time a bear got in your cabin."

"Pinto Jack and me had a mine up there," the old man said. "This was back in the fifties. Had us a little gold mine up there and a cabin tucked back in that grove of aspen. Well, one time a bear got in our cabin and . . ."

Tully sighed and stared off into the distance. Pap's ten thousandth repetition of the bear story had sent the speedometer to eighty-five. He snapped on the flashers on the light bar.

After Pap had run out the bear story, Tully told him more about Batim's phone call.

"I reckon old Batim's telling the truth," Pap said. "Hard even to guess how many people the Scraggs have killed, but I can't imagine a shrewd old fox like Batim reporting one of his own murders to you. He and those two boys of his probably filled half the prospect holes in the Hoodoos with their victims. No reason I can think of he'd report one of his own killings."

"Yeah," Tully said. "Maybe Lem or Lister might pull a stunt like that just for laughs. Can't imagine Batim doing it, though."

The old man pulled out a pack of tobacco and cigarette papers.

"No smoking in the car," Tully said.

Pap laid down a line of tobacco in a folded paper, rolled it into a skinny, crooked little cigarette, gave the paper a lick and stuck it in his mouth. He punched in the lighter on the dashboard and watched for it to pop out. "You know your great-granddaddy Beauregard Tully was the sheriff who hung Batim's great-granddaddy, Rupert Scragg?" The lighter popped out. Pap lit his cigarette, stuck it in his mouth, inhaled, then replaced the lighter. He blew a stream of smoke at Tully. The smell was terrible. "Now, Rupert might or might not have been the fella who robbed the stage and killed the driver and a passenger. Beauregard said it didn't make too much difference either way, because even if Rupert hadn't done any robbing or murdering yet, he'd get around to it sooner or later, because that's what Scraggs did. So it was kinda what you might call a preemptive hanging." Pap smiled.

Tully shook his head. "Ah, for the good old days. I don't imagine a preemptive hanging ever occurred to you, did it, Pap?"

The dark little eyes hardened. "Can't say it never did. I might have hung a few juries, too, given the opportunity."

Tully glanced over to see if the old man showed signs of having committed a pun, but he seemed dead serious.

"Worst thing ever invented," Pap went on. "Trial by a jury of your peers. What does that mean, anyway? You try a bank robber, you got to round up twelve bank robbers for a jury? Ha! Ain't no such thing as a jury of your peers, unless, of course, you happen to be an idiot. Then there's a pretty good chance you'll get a jury of your peers."

Tully laughed. "You may be right about that."

"Of course I am," the old man said, flicking his cigarette ash onto the floor. "Hey, what's that up ahead?"

"Looks like car trouble," Tully said. "Better check it out."

Two old pickup trucks were parked one behind the other on the edge of the highway. They were headed in the direction of Blight City. The front pickup had its hood up. Four men were gathered around it. Two of them were leaning into the engine compartment, while the others offered advice. They all looked like cowboys.

They wore weathered jeans and denim jackets with cowboy hats and boots. They seemed a bit uneasy when they saw the sheriff's emblem and light bar on the Explorer. Tully stretched his lanky frame out the door and did his calm, sheriff's mosey over to them. The men watched him with apprehension.

"Howdy," Tully greeted them.

"Howdy," they replied in ragged unison, no less nervous.

"So what seems to be the trouble?"

"Don't know," one of the cowboys said, straightening up from the engine compartment. "We stopped to take a leak, and then she wouldn't start again."

Tully leaned over and looked at the engine, as if he might have a clue. The men watched him hopefully, little realizing the sheriff couldn't tell a carburetor from a cabaret. "Hmmm," he said thoughtfully, straightening up and placing his hands on his hips. Then he turned and gestured for Pap to come over.

The old man moseyed across the highway. Tully had studied moseying from him. Pap stared silently into the engine compartment for a couple of minutes. Then he said to one of the two older men, "What's your name?"

"Barton. Pete Barton."

"You got a bottle of water in your truck, Pete?"

Barton frowned. The other men glanced at each other.

Tully pretended he knew what was going on.

"Got a thermos with some cold coffee in it," Pete Barton said.

"That'll do."

One of the younger men got the thermos of coffee and handed it to Pap.

The old man poured a bit of coffee on each of the battery terminals. "Now try it."

One of the younger men got in and hit the starter. The truck roared to life.

"Any time you stop to pee and your truck won't go afterwards, you try this," Pap told Barton. "If you don't have coffee, you might pee on the battery, although, now that I think about it, I probably wouldn't recommend that."

Tully nodded, as if to say, "That's right."

"You get into Blight City," Pap went on, "you might see about cleaning up those battery terminals and tightening the bolts on the clamps."

Barton grinned at him. "First time I ever seen coffee used to start a rig."

Pap laughed. "Starts me every morning. You boys look familiar. You work up in Famine?"

"Work for Vern Littlefield on his ranch. At least we did. Worked nine years for him. But Vern's foreman, a guy named Mitchell, let us go this morning."

"How come?"

"Said they didn't need us anymore. Wanted us off the ranch before noon."

"What about the cattle?"

"Going to get rid of the cattle and start growing grapes."

"Grapes!"

"Yep. Said there's more money in grapes than cattle these days."

"Nine years," Tully said. "Seems kind of odd Littlefield wouldn't tell you himself instead of letting his foreman do it."

"I thought so. I guess Vern went off on an elk hunt all by himself last night. Anyway, didn't seem quite like him, not to see us off. But you know how rich folks are."

Tully looked at Pap. "Yeah, I do," he said. "Where you boys headed now?"

"Texas. West Texas. They got fire ants there now but I don't think they got any grapes or plan to have any. Never thought I'd be glad to see a fire ant."

Tully thought for a moment, tugging on the corner of his mustache. The men watched him in silence. Pap handed the thermos back to Barton and slammed down the hood.

Tully said, "You know we had a murder up in Famine last night. I can't have you fellas leaving right now. You've got to stay on a while longer. Tell you what. There's the Pine Creek Motel in Blight City. You know where it is?"

"Yep."

"The owner is a friend of mine. Well, she was once. Anyway, I'll give her a call and she'll put you up for a couple days or so. The county will pay all your expenses. Don't mind the lady's moaning and groaning. Her name is Ms. Simmons. Janet Simmons. You can eat your meals at Granny's Café across the street. Won't cost you anything there either, except a little indigestion."

"We didn't have anything to do with a murder," Barton said. "Didn't even hear about it, maybe because we lived in a house on the other side of the ranch. But a couple of days with all expenses paid, that sounds like a vacation to me."

The other cowboys smiled, as if they too could use a little paid vacation time. One of the younger men said, "You gonna pay our bar bill, too?"

Tully had to give that some thought, putting considerable strain on the corner of his mustache. "Okay," he said finally. "One night."

A couple of the cowboys nudged each other. Tully knew he had made a mistake.

Tully and Pap watched the two trucks go off down the road toward Blight City.

"First time I ever started a truck with coffee," Pap said.

"I thought it might be."

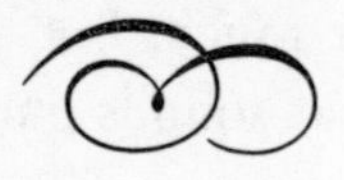

Chapter 3

For the past ten minutes they had been driving past the Littlefield ranch, which stretched to the mountains on both sides of the highway. A herd of Littlefield cattle, hundreds of black dots, grazed beneath the distant foothills of the Snowy Mountains.

"How much land you suppose Littlefield's got now?" Pap asked.

"Oh, I think he's down to his last forty or fifty thousand acres."

"That's a pity. Back in the good old days, when Rupert Scragg was hanged by Great Grampa, the ranch was so big it had its own town for its employees. When most of the field hands started getting their own vehicles and living off the ranch, Vern's grandfather burned down the whole town except for the hotel. He'd built the hotel for visitors to the ranch. Look off over there toward the mountains. That's where the town was. You can still see the hotel."

Tully looked to where the old man was pointing. A two-story frame building poked up out of tall grass beyond a distant meadow. He had driven this highway hundreds of times and never before noticed the building. "Must have had a lot of visitors, to have his own hotel."

"Reckon he did. The town had its own cemetery, too. It's on that grassy knoll up behind the hotel. Speaking of cemeteries, I guess old Vern got himself a new young bride."

"Is that right? I'm not tapped into the gossip in this part of the county, like some people I could mention."

"Well, you should be," Pap said. "A good sheriff is a good snoop."

By ten o'clock they had driven the thirty miles between Blight City and the little town of Famine. The name had originated with the first prospectors to arrive in the valley after gold had been discovered in the late 1800s. The name derived from their having nearly starved to death during the first winter. By the 1940s, the gold had played out. The name once again became appropriate and had remained so ever since. Somehow a population of two-hundred-odd souls still clung to life there, nobody knew how, nor why, not the least themselves.

Tully shut off the light bar and slowed to twenty-five as he drove through the town. The highway served as the town's main street. On one side was a small brick grade school and its playgrounds, the barnlike Famine General Store, and Ed's Gas-N-Grub, the town's only gas station. Across the highway were Burk's Hardware and Feed, Hurter's Grocery, LouLou's Restaurant and the Gold Nugget tavern. The Gold Nugget was thought of by Tully as the standard locale for picking up the perpetrators of friendly killings. And often the victims, too. It was handy that way.

"I reckon Vern Littlefield still runs this town," Pap said. "It's practically surrounded by the ranch. He's gotta be getting pretty old, though."

"Sixties," Tully said. "Vern looked in good shape the last time I saw him, but that was at Dave's House of Fry. So you never can tell."

Dave's House of Fry prided itself on offering "The World's Best and Biggest Chicken-Fried Steak." It was located three miles up the highway from Famine. Tully figured Dave Perkins, the owner, was probably Idaho's most prolific serial killer, cholesterol being his weapon of choice. As far as he knew, pie and coffee were the only things served at the café unfried, and he wasn't entirely sure about those.

"Littlefield and Batim Scragg still divide up this part of the county between them?" Tully asked.

"Probably. I think the arrangement is, Scragg steals from Littlefield and Littlefield steals from everybody else."

As they passed the city limits, Tully turned the light bar on and set the cruise control back at eighty-five, swerving out around a logging truck as he did so. Pap stiffened in his seat and then relaxed again as they moved back into the right lane. Another logging truck, this one bulging with a load of skinny logs, sped past in the opposite direction. "Been driving long?" Pap asked.

"Quite a while," Tully said. "I can always let you out and you can hitch a ride home, you want."

"Naw, hitching's too dangerous these days. I'll take my chances with you, poor as they are. By the way, I hear your girlfriend broke up with you. How come?"

"The usual reasons. Inattentive, insensitive, inane and gross. I think there were some other reasons, but I can't remember them. That was practically six weeks ago."

"Women!" Pap said. "I don't think I'll ever understand them."

"I thought you did. You've had enough of them."

"What are you talking about?" Pap said. "You don't never have enough women. But I guess I had my share. I loves them all, I truly do. The only one I ever really loved, though, was your mother. Which one was she, now?"

Tully glanced at the old man. He could never be sure whether he was joking. "Rose—Katherine Rose," he said.

"Oh, I knew it was Rose all right. Prettiest brunette I ever laid eyes on."

"Redhead."

"What?"

"Red. She had red hair. How would you know, anyway? You were never around all the time I was growing up. Other kids had dads that took them hunting and fishing, but not me."

"That's right. And have you ever had the common human decency to thank me? No, you have not! Never once! Can you imagine how you would have turned out if you had me hanging around all the time, dragging you out to go fishing and hunting? Why, it's almost too horrible even to contemplate."

Tully whipped the Explorer out around a pickup truck and blasted the driver with his horn for failing to yield to a law officer's vehicle with flashing lights. Pap sucked his latest cigarette—flaming—halfway to his lips. "You got that hitching-back-to-town offer still open?" he asked.

"Nope. You had your chance."

"We're coming to the Scragg ranch," Pap said. "You might want to stop driving like a maniac and slow down."

Unlike the Littlefield ranch, where the house and outbuildings were set back against the mountains, the main Scragg buildings were all clustered out near the highway, possibly, as Pap explained, in case the Scraggs needed to make a fast getaway, as they often did. Any paint on the two-story ranch house was now a distant memory. In addition to whatever living quarters existed inside the main house, two ancient mobile homes squatted in the weedy backyard. Tully guessed that Lem and Lister, and whatever wives or girlfriends they might have, lived in the mobile homes. Corrals, loading chutes, barns, silos, coops and ancient outbuildings staggered off toward the mountains. All were weathered gray and in disrepair, obviously no longer in use.

Someone had built a bonfire out in the yard and assorted male Scraggs and neighbors from the area stood and hunkered around it drinking beer out of cans. Lem and Lister, both of them closing in on forty, slumped in straight-back chairs they had apparently dragged out of the house. Their long legs stretched out in front of them toward the fire. Their scraggly blond hair hung down the backs of the chairs. Batim leaned against a post that seemed to have no other function than to hold him up. Buck Toole's red Explorer was parked in the driveway but there was no sign of the deputy. The state patrolman hadn't arrived yet.

Tully got out and moseyed over toward the group. Stone-faced, the Scraggs stared at him. In an instant, Lister was out of his chair and in front of Tully. He pointed over the sheriff's shoulder. "What's that old man doing here? You get him out of here!"

"Stay out of his face, Lister," Batim said, still leaning against his post. He was chewing on a wooden matchstick.

"I told you to get him out of here!" Lister shouted.

A familiar numb feeling moved up Tully's right arm.

He turned and looked back. Pap was standing next to the Explorer, the .30-30 rifle resting back over his right shoulder. His right hand was through the lever, his finger poised just outside the trigger guard. Tully turned. Lister was lying flat on his back on the ground in front of him, his long greasy hair splayed out like a halo around his head. His eyes were glazed and blood trickled from his mouth. This sort of thing always made Tully nervous. He had no recollection of hitting Lister, but he knew better than to let on.

Still leaning against the post, Batim shook his head in disgust. He spat out the matchstick. "Lister, I told you, get out of his face. He quick like that. Next time, maybe you'll listen to your pa. Anyway, Bo, don't pay Lister no mind. A boy's got to learn."

Tully looked among the astonished Scraggs, none of whom moved to help Lister. "I see my deputy's car, but I don't see Buck anywhere," he said. "Any of you boys be kind enough to tell me where he might be?"

An elderly man wearing an earflap cap, possibly a neighboring Scragg, pushed himself up from his hunker at the fire and pointed out into the pasture beyond the buildings. "He's out there, Sheriff."

Tully looked out at the pasture. "I don't see him."

"That little stand of trees about halfway out? Your deputy is up one of them trees. That tan patch. You can see the sun flashing off his badge every so often."

Tully squinted. "What's he doing up there?"

"Look just off to the left and kinda behind the trees. You see the bull? Once in a while he paws up some dirt."

"Oh yeah." Tully tugged on the corner of his mustache. "I don't suppose anyone mentioned to Buck there was a bull out in that pasture."

"I don't think he asked," Lem Scragg said with mock solemnity.

The group of Scraggs and neighbors chuckled among themselves.

Tully turned and called to Pap. "Bring that thirty-thirty up here!"

"Good idea," Pap said.

"Hold on there, Bo," Batim said, pushing away from his post. "That bull's worth twenty thousand dollars." Then he leaned back against the post. "But shoot it if you want. It ain't mine, it's Littlefield's. Critter keeps jumping the fence onto my property. Actually, you'd be doing me a favor to shoot it."

"I wasn't planning on shooting the bull," Tully said. "I was planning on shooting Buck. Now you tell one of your kinfolk here to get that bull out of the pasture, before I start shooting Scraggs."

"Oh, all right," Batim said. "Lem, run that bull into the corral."

"Why me, Pa?" Lem remained sprawled in his chair.

"'Cause I say so, that's why!"

Languid as a cat, Lem got up and stripped off his dirty shirt. He climbed through a pole fence and walked out into the pasture, waving the shirt. "Here, bull! Here, bull!" he called out.

The bull came for him, running hard and fast. At the last minute Lem darted into a corral and went up and over a high pole fence. The bull followed him into the corral. It slid to a stop and stood there glaring through the fence at its intended victim. While it bellowed, pawed dirt and shook strings of slobber from its muzzle, several Scraggs closed a pole gate behind it. Lem strolled back to the group, put his shirt back on, settled himself in his chair, stretched his legs out toward the fire and picked up his can of beer.

"Durn bull," Batim said. "Wish Littlefield would manage to keep his animals on his own property."

"Yeah," Pap said. He was still holding the rifle, but had come up alongside of Tully. "Otherwise, a person might get accused of rustling."

"That's right," Batim agreed.

Out in the grove of trees, Buck slid to the ground and walked back across the pasture. He stooped and picked up his gun, which he stuck back in his holster.

"I suppose you want to see the body," Batim said.

"That's what we came for," Tully said.

"Well, it's that dark shape over the fence out beyond the trees. There's a cross fence between here and it. The bull couldn't get to the body."

"Good," Tully said.

Lister was sitting up now, gingerly feeling his jaw with one hand. Tully stepped around him and headed out into the pasture. Pap followed. The Scraggs turned and looked at Batim.

"Y'all stay where you are," he told them. "I reckon that's a crime scene out there."

Chapter 4

By the time the deputy and Tully met, Buck was still working his way through his rather large vocabulary of profanity, some of the words running to twelve or more letters. Tully had heard most of the words before, but he thought Buck might be creating some new ones for the occasion.

"Bull nearly got me," he told the sheriff. "I fired a couple of rounds at him and missed and then took off for the trees. Just barely made it up one of them. Almost froze to death up there, too."

Tully shook his head in disgust. "I don't want to hear it."

They waited for Pap to catch up, then opened a wire gate and made their way out to the body. As Batim had indicated, the dead man was wearing a dark-blue pin-stripe suit, a shiny black shoe on one foot and only a black sock on the other foot. He looked to be about forty-five or fifty, but in good shape. There were two tiny black holes in the back of his jacket.

"Nice suit," Pap said.

"Yeah," Tully said. "Don't see many like it around Blight County." He reached inside the man's jacket, pulled out a slender billfold and opened it. "The fellow seems to be Nicholas Holt from Los Angeles, California." He ran his hand into a pants pocket and pulled out a wad of folded hundred-dollar bills fastened with a gold money clip.

"Well, this tells me one thing," he said.

"He's rich?" Buck said.

"Maybe that, too. But for sure, he wasn't killed by one of the Scraggs, and they sure haven't been out here checking the body. Maybe Batim actually learned something over the years."

Pap squatted down and studied the ground near the body.

"See anything?" Tully asked.

"A couple of tracks. Looks like he was really moving when he hit the fence. Got a couple of faint shoe marks five or six feet apart. The foot with the sock on it didn't make much of a track. The ground's pretty hard."

"Somebody was after him. This guy was hunted down. How far across to that other fence you reckon?"

"Hundred yards or so," Pap said.

"Probably hit with a semiautomatic, don't you think?"

Pap straightened up and blew on his hands to warm them. "Probably. I'd guess both slugs hit him just as he got to the fence. Pop pop! Otherwise, the first one would have knocked him down out in the pasture. Must have used a rifle at that distance. Otherwise, he was one terrific pistol shot, to put two bullets in this guy that close together."

"I don't get it," Buck said. "The Scraggs say they didn't hear a thing during the night."

"What Scraggs say doesn't mean much," Tully said.

Pap studied the far fence. "I wouldn't be surprised if he was shot from there," he said, pointing. "Full moon last night. Pretty bright out. Could have shot without a night scope. Probably had a night scope anyway."

"Wouldn't hurt if we got ourselves a tracker," Tully said. "See if we can pick up a trail of some kind."

"How about Dave Perkins?" Buck said. "He claims to be an Indian."

"Dave is about as Indian as I am," Pap said. "That doesn't stop him from talking about opening a casino on his reservation."

Tully turned from examining the body. "His reservation? What's his reservation?"

"I guess it's what Dave's House of Fry sits on," Buck said. "About five acres. Dave claims not only is it the 'Home of the World's Best and Biggest Chicken-Fried Steak,' it's also the world's smallest Indian reservation."

"I suppose he has a tribe, too," Tully said.

"Oh yeah," Buck said. "The Dave Tribe."

"Figures. Buck, go see if you can get him out here. Tell him the Sheriff's Department will even pay him for his services this time."

"They paying for my services, too?" Pap said.

"No."

"How did I guess that?"

Chapter 5

Tully slipped the roll of cash back into the dead man's pocket and the billfold back into the suit jacket.

"I hate to see a law officer do something that stupid," Pap said.

Tully smiled. "Not many guys around here carry their cash like that. A wad in their pocket."

"For one thing, they don't have cash like that," Pap said. "If they did, they'd still keep it in their billfold and the billfold in their hip pocket. They keep all their money and important papers in their billfolds. Most of them look like they got some kind of growth on their butt even without the cash."

"So why do you figure a guy like this would be out here in the middle of the night?"

"Beats me. He sure don't look like a rustler, but there ain't nothing around here except a bunch of cows. Hey, here comes the new medical examiner now, I bet."

A white Chevy Suburban bumped across the pasture.

The vehicle stopped a few feet away. A trim, tall woman with shoulder-length, dark hair got out. She wore dark-rimmed glasses, a blue insulated jacket over jeans and leather boots. She was in fact quite a bit prettier than Tully's perky secretary. She held out her gloved hand.

"Hi, Sheriff, I'm Susan Parker. We haven't had a chance to meet."

Tully shook her hand. Her grip was firm. "Call me Bo," he said. "Nice to meet you, Susan. This sorry old character here is my father, Eldon Tully, former sheriff of Blight County. Everybody calls him Pap."

"Hi, Pap," she said, stepping around the body and shaking the old man's hand.

"Good you showed up," Pap told her. "We got a dead body here we don't know what to do with."

Susan took off her leather gloves and pulled on a pair of latex gloves. "I've seen quite a few dead bodies. This is the first one I've come across in a cow pasture, though."

"Me, too," said Tully. "Most of the dead bodies I find are in our local drinking establishments. With the killer at the bar bragging about his work."

"I see he was shot," she said. "Might have been from a semiautomatic, with two bullet holes tight together like that."

Tully gave Pap a look. "Yeah, that's about what we figured. Probably shot sometime during the night, maybe using a night-vision scope on a small-caliber rifle. The Scraggs claim they didn't hear a thing."

"You believe those people?" she said.

"Not ordinarily," Tully said. "But as old Batim says, if it had been one of them there wouldn't have been an awkward situation like this. He means they would have dropped the body down a prospect hole or something equally efficient."

"Why didn't he do that anyway?"

"Don't know. He probably thought about it, all right, but this way there's a certain amount of entertainment value for him and his clan. I'm pretty sure Batim didn't let any of the Scraggs come near the body."

Susan snapped a dozen photos of the body while Tully watched.

"If you'll give me a hand," she said, "let's see if we can lift him off the fence."

Pap watched as Susan and Tully lifted the body from the fence and laid it out on the ground face up.

She's a lot stronger than she looks, Tully thought. He watched as she went through the man's pockets. She looked at the driver's license. "From Los Angeles," she said. "Nicholas Holt. Born October 1959. Forty-one years old."

Then she pulled out the wad of hundred-dollar bills. "Whewee! I guess we can rule out robbery as the motive. That Rolex on his wrist is probably real, too."

"I can tell you this," Tully said. "If the Scraggs had shot him, the money and the watch would be gone for sure. They probably had something to do with it one way or another, but I don't think they're the ones that killed him."

She unbuttoned the man's shirt and pulled it back. "The bullets didn't exit. That's odd. We should be able to get some markings off them to match with a weapon."

Pap spoke up. "Might be a twenty-two rifle. Kind of odd for a murder weapon but handy. Probably every house in the county has one."

Back by the ranch house, Buck's Explorer pulled through the gate and started working its way across the pasture.

"Buck's back," Pap said. "Wish my driver had had enough sense to drive out here." He looked over at Bo, who glared back at him. "Because I'm near froze to death."

"Good heavens!" Susan said. "No wonder you're cold. Neither of you is wearing a coat."

"Coats are for sissies," Tully said. "And pretty ladies, of course."

Susan gave him a tiny smile. She walked over to the Suburban and came back with an aluminum case. She took out an instrument that looked like a meat thermometer and stuck it into the liver of the corpse.

"Cripes!" Pap said. "Let me know when you're going to do stuff like that so I can look away."

Susan smiled at him. "Some sheriff you must have been."

"I didn't go poking dead bodies with sharp instruments, if that's what you mean. Mostly what I did was turn them into dead bodies in the first place. It's not so gross."

Tully was glad the old man hadn't told her how many dead bodies he had done.

"I'm sorry," she said, "but I may be able to give you

an approximate time of death, even cold as it was last night."

The Explorer pulled up behind the Suburban. Buck and Dave Perkins got out. Dave, a chunky sixty-year-old, wore his long gray hair in a single braid down his back. He wore a folded red bandana around his head, well-scuffed cowboy boots, jeans and a red-and-black-checked mackinaw over a blue wool shirt open at the collar. Tully introduced them to Susan.

"Buck Toole is one of my deputies. Dave Perkins here owns my favorite restaurant in the whole country. He used to be a pretty good tracker. We'll see if he still is."

"All us Indians are good trackers," Dave said. "Show us a bent blade of grass and we can tell you the person's height, weight, country of origin and telephone number."

Susan laughed. "Well, that's certainly impressive."

"Yes, it is," Dave said. He took out a glasses case and put on a pair of wire-framed spectacles. "These are special tracking glasses."

"I understand," Susan said, smiling broadly.

Nice teeth, Tully thought.

Dave walked the length of the body until he got to the feet. Then he squatted down and studied the man's shoe and sock. He stood up and stared back across the pasture to another open field backed by a wooded area. "That field and that woods over there, I think that's part of the Littlefield ranch. The Scragg ranch got itself surrounded by Littlefield years ago."

"Looks like the shooter might have come from over

there in the woods," Tully said. "Probably the victim, too. Any road over there?"

"An old mine road but not much else. Used to be a bridge over a little crick, but it washed out years ago. You can drive across when the water's low like it is now. The road used to go up to the Last Hope Mine, but the owners dynamited the mine shut after it closed. Then they plowed up a berm to block the road."

"Pap and I'll drive over there and look around," Tully said. "You see if you can pick up any trail and we'll meet you at the road. Buck, you stay with Susan, in case she needs help."

Tully and Pap started walking back to the Explorer.

"Not a bad looker," Pap said, glancing back at the medical examiner.

"Dave's all right but nothing special," Tully said.

Pap responded with a seven-letter obscenity.

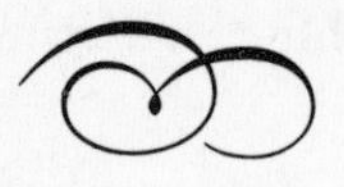

Chapter 6

The crowd at Batim's house had diminished to three. None of the Scraggs was out in the yard. A couple of women and several small children watched them out a window. The men in the yard were apparently neighbors, curious about the murder.

"How's it going?" Tully said.

"Not bad," one of the men said. "Hear you got a murder out there, Sheriff."

"Appears that way," Tully said.

He and Pap got in the Explorer and drove off.

Pap rolled and lit a cigarette.

"I liked the way you put down that Lister Scragg," he said. "You're about as quick a man as I've ever seen."

"Thanks. So what was it between you and Lister that got him so riled up? I'm the one put him in prison."

"Kind of a long story," Pap said. "Lister must be about forty now. It would have been fifteen or so years ago. That boy does hold a grudge. It was the second time that he'd put that itsy-bitsy wife of his in the hospital. But she refused to press charges. Scared, I guess. He'd blacked both her eyes and broke her jaw, but she was afraid of him. I was so mad I drove out to the Scragg ranch and walked in the house. They was all sitting around the dinner table. I grabbed Lister, jerked him out of his chair and threw him up against the wall. Put the cuffs on him in front, because I knew what I was gonna do. Old Batim was shouting, 'You got a warrant, you got a warrant? What's the charge?' I told him to shut up, that he didn't know anything about the law just because he'd been in prison a couple of times. I pushed Lister out the door and into my pickup. He's yelling and hollering about his rights, and I says, 'I'm driving you into the next county. You ain't got no rights over there.' I drove him up the West Branch Road way out in the woods till we come to that old horse-packing camp out there. The meat pole for hanging deer carcasses is about eight feet high, and I hauled Lister out of the truck, tied a rope to the handcuffs and tossed it up over the top of the meat pole. Then I pulled the pickup around to the other side and tied the rope to the pickup's winch. I winched Lister up till he was standing on his tippy toes.

"It's dark by now so I have the lights turned on him. He's yelling and bellowing and waking up all the coyotes in the entire canyon and they're all howling. A big October moon was just coming up, probably about like last night, and it's beautiful, but it's all kinds of eerie, too. I walked over to the river bank and cut me an eight-foot willow a little thicker than my thumb. Then I sat down on the bumper of the truck and started to shave the bark off that willow with my knife, Lister straining around and watching every stroke. 'What you aimin' to do with that willow?' Lister croaked out. I said, 'You ever heard of caning, Lister?' He said no he hadn't, which is about what I expected, because Lister ain't never heard of nothing. Lem is pretty intelligent but Lister is dumb as stone. So I explained it to him. I says I ain't never experienced it personally myself but I read an account about a fella who did, over in one of them Asian countries, and he said the pain of the first whack exploded like a bomb in his head, and then it got a whole lot worse from then on. Well, you never heard such carrying on as come from Lister when I told him that. By then I had all the bark whittled off the willow and I got up and went around and undid Lister's belt and let his pants drop around his ankles. He was wearing long johns with that flap in the back that buttons up. I undid the buttons so that his skinny old rear end was sticking out there in the moonlight pale as a peeled egg. By now he's dancing around on his tippy toes and really whooping it up. So I stepped over to one side with my willow cane held up in both hands and . . ."

"I don't want to hear this!" Tully said.

"You're gonna hear it, so shut up and listen!"

Pap took a final drag on his cigarette and crushed it out in the ashtray.

"It will do you some good, Bo," he said. "So I told Lister, 'I figure you got at least fifteen licks coming for each time you put that wife of yours in the hospital. But right now I'm putting them all on hold. If I ever hear tell of you laying a finger on her again, I'm gonna bring you out here and collect all of them plus another fifteen. You hear?' Lister kinda nodded that he'd heard. All the way driving back to the Scragg ranch he sat slumped in the seat like a big pile of mush. He never said a word but every once in a while he let out this little moan, like I had beat him half to death. I pulled up in the Scragg yard, took off the cuffs and shoved him out. He just laid there on the ground, like he was so tuckered out he couldn't move."

"I'm about that tuckered out myself," Tully said, "and I just heard the story."

"About the time his wife healed up, she ran off with some fella she'd met at the hospital. Probably never even knew the favor I done her. She was a pretty little thing, cute as a bug's ear."

Tully slowed the Explorer and pointed to an opening in the brush. A small piece of orange fluorescent tape was tied to a branch near the opening.

"Looks like somebody marked the road," he said, pointing to the tape. He could see car tracks disappearing into the brush.

"Hunters sometimes use that tape to mark the way back to a deer they got down," Pap said.

"Yeah," Tully said. "But this time I think it only marks the road."

"Fresh car tracks, probably made last night, all right," Pap said.

"You sure we want to find out?"

"No, but I expect we better."

Chapter 7

Tully eased the Explorer through the brush that covered the road's entrance. Within a hundred yards, he came to a stream. He punched the button to engage the Explorer's four-wheel drive. The SUV plowed through the shallow water and up the bank on the far side. Here the brush closed in even tighter, like a leafy tunnel. The woods were thick with snowberry, Oregon grape, wild rose, alders, birch, quaking aspen and young cottonwoods. Tully thought he might come over here in the summer to look for dewberries. His mother still made dewberry jam every summer.

"Good place to get brush scratches on a new vehicle," Pap said.

"Scratched up this rig long ago," Tully said.

"The car ahead of us probably wasn't. I'd never do this to a car, less'n it happened to be a rental. Or owned by the county. There's still only one track. You know what that means."

"There was only one car, I suppose."

"No, it means they're still up here. Or found another way out. And I don't think there's another way out."

Pap held the .30-30 upright between his legs. He worked the lever, jacking a shell into the chamber, then lowered the hammer back down.

Tully stopped, the wet brakes grabbing and squeaking. He took the keys from the ignition, reached over and unlocked the glove compartment. He took out the Glock and removed it from the holster. He pulled the slide back and closed it, chambering a round. "How far to the end of the road do you think?" he asked.

"I'm not sure," Pap said. "I remember it now, though. Years ago I hunted it for grouse and even then it had a big berm of dirt and rock across it just below where it started up the mountain."

"We better walk," Tully said. "I don't like the idea of driving up on whoever's in that car."

"I hate walking," Pap said.

"These could be hunters," Tully said. "But I'd rather not be a sitting target if they're not."

They got out of the Explorer and pressed the doors closed behind them. They walked up the road, ducking beneath the overhanging brush and tree limbs. The day was warming up and the frost on the brush was melting and starting to drip. Every so often an icy drip slithered down the back of Tully's neck and reminded him that he could have been wearing his cowboy hat. He noticed that his father moved through the brush effortlessly without making a sound. Occasionally he would see where a vehicle had scraped a rock in the road or taken the bark off part of a small tree growing up between the tracks. He was pretty sure it had to be a four-wheel drive. As they neared the place where the mountain rose abruptly out of the woods, he saw the shiny black shape of a car roof. He signaled to Pap. The old man nodded back. He had already seen it. Tully moved over close to him.

"Both doors are closed on this side," Pap whispered.

"Rear door is open on the left side," Tully whispered back.

"Don't hear anybody talking."

"Yeah. Pretty quiet. Move up real slow."

Tully expected an ambush at any moment. He was peering ahead through the trees and brush on each side of the road, and he was glad he had brought Pap along. Pap was old for this sort of thing but still better than most.

Pap crossed over to him and whispered. "I don't see nobody moving around."

Tully stopped and took a deep breath. "I hear birds and squirrels. I don't think there's anybody up there."

Tully and Pap moved cautiously into the clearing. The mountain reared straight up directly in front of a black Jeep Grand Cherokee. The Jeep's front bumper rested against the berm, now grown over with brush.

Bullet holes riddled the car on the right side. The back seat was empty. There was no sign of blood on the seat, but the right rear door was full of bullet holes. The glass had been shot out. No one could have avoided that spray of lead, Tully thought.

"Two dead guys in the front seat," Pap said.

He took out a handkerchief and used it to open the right front door.

"This one's got a gun," he whispered. "Never got it out of his shoulder holster."

Tully went around to the driver's side of the car. He tucked the Glock in the rear waistband of his pants, wrapped his handkerchief around his hand and opened the front door a crack. The car was still in drive and had drifted ahead until stopped by the berm. The driver was slumped against the door. Tully pushed him back into the front seat. He too had a gun in a shoulder holster. The fuel gauge was on empty. He turned off the ignition key. The headlights were on. He wrapped the handkerchief around his left hand and turned the lights off. He walked around to the front of the vehicle and opened the hood. He lay his hand on the radiator cap. He leaped back, shaking his hand and bellowing.

Pap smiled. "I thought you didn't allow your department people to use any obscenities, particularly that one."

"When they burn themselves on a radiator cap, they can," Tully said, examining his hand.

"We can stop whispering now," Pap said. "These two fellas are dead. If the killers were still here, we'd probably be dead, too."

"I guess you're right," Tully said. Even their own voices sounded a bit spooky in the silence of the woods.

The driver wore a white shirt and tie without a suit jacket.

"You think they're feds?" Tully asked.

Pap had opened the lift gate at the rear of the Jeep.

"Naw," Pap said. "Too well dressed for feds. There are two suit jackets folded up back here."

Tully was going through a billfold. "Here's a driver's license. He's from L.A., too. Probably mob. Both these fellows are pretty beefy. I bet they were bodyguards."

"Probably," Pap said.

"The guy at the fence, Holt, had to be riding in the back seat," Tully said. "He probably came flying out of the car and made it into the woods. Then one or more of the shooters hunted him down. But with all the bullets sprayed into the back seat, I can't figure out how he managed to get away."

"He probably was a lot smarter, or more suspicious, than the guys in the front seat."

Tully shut the car door and worked his way into the woods to the left of the car. He came to where someone had stood back in the trees, matting down the dried ferns.

A pool of blood glistened darkly next to the matted-down area.

"Got a lot of blood over here," Tully said.

He knew the blood couldn't have come from Holt. There was too much of it.

Pap came around the rear of the Jeep. "The grass and ferns are all trampled down back in the woods over there," he said. "You can see where the shooters stood. Two of them. They waited a good while for the Jeep to show up. I can see where they was sitting down and even laying down."

"Any other sign?"

"They left a couple of shell casings. Nine millimeter.

Probably picked up most of them but couldn't find them all in the dark."

"Yeah," Tully said. "You leave the casings where you found them?"

"Yup. Picked one up with a little stick to check the caliber. Marked each casing with a stick."

"Got to be automatics."

"Yup."

"At least we'll have the ejector and firing-pin marks on the casings to identify the murder weapons, if we ever find them."

Tully walked back to the car and bent down, looking in the driver's window. "The clothes these guys are wearing, pretty spiffy, wouldn't you say? There's nobody around here dresses like that. Shirts must have cost a hundred dollars each, probably more. I don't think anybody in all Idaho dresses like that."

"California," Pap said. "Los Angeles. Jeep's a rental from Spokane International. I checked the papers in the glove compartment. They picked it up at ten last night."

A branch cracked back in the woods. Then another one.

"Somebody's coming," Tully said.

"Probably Dave the Indian," Pap said. "I never been around anybody made so much noise walking through the woods as Dave the Indian."

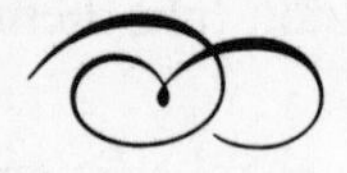

Chapter 8

Dave stopped and stared at the bullet-riddled Jeep and the bodies. "I never expected this," he said.

"Us neither," Pap said.

"You find anything?" Tully asked.

"Yep. Looks like our man was trailed by one guy," Dave said. "Shot the victim twice with a small-caliber rifle, just like you thought, Bo. Probably a two-twenty-three caliber. No exit wounds. That's according to your medical examiner. The shooter was about a hundred yards away. There's a big pasture gate there with a tall post on each end. I think he used the right post for a rest. He may have picked up one of the shell casings, but I found the other one in the tall grass near the post. It's a two-twenty-three. And I found Holt's shoe, too. The lace came loose and he must have run right out of it. I think the shooter picked it up, too, and then flung it off to one side. I marked it with a stick. Might have some prints on it. There's some soft spots out there, and I think you can get some good casts of the shooter's tracks. From the looks of them, I'd say he was wearing rubber boots."

"Good job," Tully said.

"One more thing," Dave said. "The shooter walked over and checked the victim, probably to make sure he was dead."

"Notice anything else out there?"

"Not much. Except I sure wouldn't want this killer after me. He just walked steadily along tracking the guy through the grass. Every once in a while the victim would hunker down in tall grass, maybe to rest or hide, but then he'd see this guy coming after him through the moonlight and he'd take off running. The guy just kept after him, hardly ever even breaking stride, waiting for his shot. He got it at the big gate, when the vic started to climb over that fence."

"The shooter doesn't sound anything like our local screw-ups," Tully said.

"No, he doesn't," Dave said. He glanced at his watch. "Hey, it's past lunchtime. These fellows aren't going anywhere. Let's head over to the restaurant and I'll buy you all lunch."

"Sounds good to me," Tully said. "But the county buys."

"Let me think about that," Dave said. "Okay."

Tully walked back to the Explorer and drove it up closer to the Jeep. The three of them circled the area with crime-scene tape.

Tully called the Idaho State Police on the radio to find out what had happened to the patrolman who was supposed to be sent up. The ISP radio person said he was waiting at the entrance to the Last Hope Mine Road.

Then he called Buck on the radio. "You about got things wrapped up there?"

"Yeah, Blight City Ambulance is here now. They're loading up the victim."

"Good. Take care of that, then meet us at Dave's House of Fry for lunch. Ask that medical examiner to come along, too."

"You got it."

He called the office on his cell phone. Daisy answered.

"How's it going up there?" she asked.

"Bad," he said. "Really bad. We may be up here a couple days. You'll remember to feed Wallace, right?"

"Oh, I suppose. But I'm not sticking my finger in front of him like you do."

"Good. Otherwise he might take a liking to you, show up at your house some night. Lurch still hunched over his computer?"

"Where else?"

"Tell him I need him up here right away." He gave her the directions to pass on to his CSI. "We've got blood, bodies, tracks and a car riddled with bullets. Should make him happy."

"Sounds awful," she said. "I'll get the unit on its way right now."

The ISP patrolman was sitting in his car at the entrance to the road. While Pap and Dave strung more yellow crime-scene tape across the road, Tully explained to the patrolman that they were going to grab some lunch and would be back with the medical examiner shortly. "So what happened in there?" the patrolman asked.

"It appears that three guys from Los Angeles came up here to get something, and somebody up here in Blight County didn't want them to have it. That's my guess, anyway. So the three guys from L.A. are now dead."

"The L.A. guys should have known better than to mess around up here," the patrolman said.

"I can't argue with that. Say, do me a favor, will you?"

"Sure."

"My CSI unit is going to be up here right away and . . ."

"You got a CSI unit?" the patrolman said.

"Yeah, his name is Lurch."

"Figures."

"Tell him to go directly east from the Jeep and he'll find a shell casing, a shoe and several tracks marked with sticks. He is to pick up the casing and the shoe and make some dental-stone casts of the tracks."

The cop wrote the instructions to Lurch in his notebook. "I feel like a secretary," he said.

"You look like one, too," Tully said.

He, Pap and Dave got in the Explorer and headed to the restaurant.

Dave said, "How do you fasten this seat belt, anyway?"

"Funny," Pap said. "I was going to ask the same thing."

Chapter 9

Tully, Pap and Dave were seated at a table in the back of the restaurant when Buck showed up with Susan. Even though she was tall, she seemed tiny alongside the hulking deputy.

Buck said, "I would've stopped and beat on Scraggs awhile, but I thought Susan here might not like the violence."

Pap was the only one at the table to welcome the lady properly. He rose and tipped his Stetson.

"You are a true gentleman, Pap," she said, beaming. "Not many of you left."

"I don't think she would be all that bothered by a little violence, Buck," Tully said.

"A little beating might have taught the Scraggs some manners," Susan said.

Tully wasn't at all sure this comment wasn't meant for him and Dave. But he didn't care. He was tired already and the day was just getting started. "It's your restaurant, Dave," he said. "What do you recommend?"

"Let me see. Hmmm. I think I'd recommend the chicken-fried steak. Hear it's the best in the world. It comes with gravy over the steak and hash browns."

"The hash browns still got that sheen of grease on them?"

"Still do. Make them by hand right here from fresh Idaho spuds. Cover them with lots of the best grease money can buy."

"Good."

Noticing Susan rather thoughtfully perusing the menu, Tully wondered if she would go for the chicken-fried steak, too. She did. Might be my kind of woman after all, he thought. On the other hand, he wasn't sure he could get used to a woman who matter-of-factly shoved a thermometer into a dead man's liver.

A waitress named Shirley came and took their orders. Afterwards, Dave told Susan and Buck about the second murder scene.

"Yeah," Tully said, "a pool of blood on the ground back in the woods a little ways from the Jeep. Maybe Holt came out of the back seat firing a pistol and hit somebody just by chance. I don't think the victim was a shooter, because none of the bullet holes in the Jeep came from that side. Maybe just an interested observer. Then Holt kept going. Dave traced the track from the fence to the Jeep, but never came across the pistol."

"Right, no pistol," Dave said. "So I figure Holt emptied it and dropped it and it was picked up by whoever shot him. The tracker went right for him, like he knew Holt wasn't armed anymore. Or maybe never."

Susan said, "You can tell that from the tracks?"

"Pretty much. He wasn't dodging round like somebody was taking shots at him or like he expected the guy to."

Tully said, "We at least know who the men in the car were and that they came from Los Angeles. But what were people like that doing up here in Blight County? And on the Last Hope Road of all places?"

"Got to be a setup," Buck said. "No other reason somebody would drive back on that road. I can't guess who might have done it, but the Scraggs come to mind."

"Pretty hard to believe the Scraggs didn't have something to do with it," Pap said. "On the other hand, why would Batim call Bo to tell him he had a dead man over one of his fences?"

"Maybe because the trail led right to that fence," Tully said. "And there's no way they could have cleaned up all the blood at the fence. Batim knows we'd tie the guy on the fence to the guys in the woods, even if the body was gone."

Two waitresses returned with their orders. The talk at the table stopped. One of the waitresses, blond and voluptuous, suddenly blurted out, "Why, Pap Tully! I thought that was you under that black Stetson."

Pap, obviously pleased, grinned broadly. "Had to give the boys a hand, Deedee," he said. "Got some unfortunate business up here north of Famine."

"Oh, you don't have to be so secretive, Pap." She reached out, lifted his Stetson and mussed his white thicket of hair in a gesture Tully thought suspiciously familiar. "Everybody in town's heard all about the bodies in the woods and all. It's pretty creepy, hunh? Nothing like that ever happened around Famine before."

"Everybody knows about the bodies?" Tully said. "How does everybody know?"

"Well, somebody probably mentioned it down at the gas station. You know how it is, Dave, you want everyone in town to know the news, you mention it at the gas station."

"You bet," Dave said.

Susan said, "You may want to check in at the gas station, Sheriff. Maybe you can find out who the ambushers are, too?"

Tully ignored the twinkle in her eyes. "I wouldn't be surprised," he said, and dug into his hash browns and gravy. This will probably kill me, he thought. Good, though.

"You been out to see Vern Littlefield yet?" Buck asked.

"No," Tully answered. "But I'm going out there to talk to him right after lunch. Been a long time since I've seen Vern. I worked for him summers when I was a kid, before I went off to the university."

"What did you do for him?" Pap asked.

"Built fences. I guess Vern figured the fences would keep the Scraggs from rustling his cattle."

"That sure didn't work, did it?" Dave said.

"No," Tully said, "it didn't. That's why I later sent both the Scragg boys, Lister and Lem, off to prison. Rustling."

"Prison didn't seem to do them much good," Pap said.

"I'll be darned," Buck said.

"What?" Tully said.

"You went to college, Bo?"

"Don't hold it against him," Pap said, grinning. "He didn't learn nothing except how to paint pictures. They got a bunch of them up on the walls of the courthouse right now."

"Why, I saw them," Buck said. He seemed about ready to offer a criticism but then thought better of it. "These sure are good hash browns, Dave."

Tully glanced at Susan. He could tell there was at least one person at the table impressed he'd been to college.

"I haven't seen your pictures yet," she said.

"I have to warn you," Tully said, "that display has caused a virtual explosion of art criticism in Blight County. Folks who previously came out of the hills only to vote against school-bond issues come to town at least twice a month now, just to voice their criticism of the sheriff's pictures."

"Hey," Dave said, "I think Bo's pictures show a lot of promise. The colors are real nice. If his art classes had just taught him something about perspective, they'd be fine."

"Is that why all your animals look like they're about to fall out of their pastures?" Pap said.

"Basically, that's it," said Dave. "No perspective."

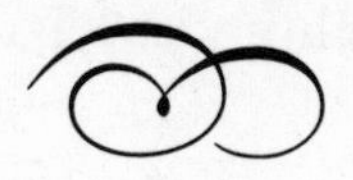

Chapter 10

After lunch, Dave stayed at the café, and Susan and Buck headed out to the old mining road. Tully and Pap stopped by the gas station. Ed Grange, who owned and operated the station, was out cleaning the windshield of a car being gassed up at one of the two pumps. At one end of the station were shelves of groceries, along with coolers for milk, sodas and beer. A counter ran half the length of the station. In front of the counter was an open area furnished with tables, chairs and a wood stove. A young woman stood behind the counter at the cash register. She looked too young to be working at the station. Tully wondered why she wasn't in school. She greeted them with a quick little smile when they came in. They pulled up chairs next to the fire.

"There's something you don't see much anymore," Pap commented.

"What's that?" Tully said, thinking about the girl at the cash register.

"A car getting its windshield cleaned at a gas station."

"That's because Blight County is thirty years back in time, and Famine is at least fifty years back."

"Ed still charges a dollar and a half a gallon for gas," Pap said. "I guess he's not that far back in time."

"So how much did gas cost when you were a kid, Pap?" Tully thought he should ask, just to be sociable, because he knew he was about to be told anyway.

"Back in the forties, everything cost fifteen cents," Pap said. "Didn't make no difference what, a hamburger, a pound of bacon, a gallon of gas. I don't know why fifteen cents was the magic number, but it was."

Tully expressed the appropriate amazement.

Ed put the finishing touches on the windshield, then came into the station and shook hands. "Pap complaining about the price of gas?" he said.

"Naw," Tully said. "He was just telling me how nice it was back in the olden days, back when folks plugged an artery they got death instead of a bypass. The doctor got fifteen cents."

"Didn't say nothing like that," Pap said. "But in some ways it was better back then. What do you think, Ed?"

Ed took off his hat and hung it on a peg near the stove. The few hairs on his head were combed over from ear to ear and glued to his scalp with some kind of spray. He wore clean striped overalls with a blue work shirt showing at the neck. "I think you're right about that, Pap. Seems to me everything is going haywire these days."

"Which brings me to the problem at hand," Tully

said, tugging on the corner of his mustache. "Deedee down at the café tells us that everyone in town knows about the killing out on the old mine road."

"Reckon that's true. I figure it takes maybe an hour for a newsbreak here at the station to reach everyone in town."

"Newsbreak?" Tully said. "I thought this was a gas station, not a radio station. Anyway, who dropped the word here?"

"Lem Scragg. There were three or four guys hanging around shooting the breeze when Lem come in and said there was a dead guy up at the ranch and he'd heard there were two more over at the Last Hope Mine Road. Next thing I know there was just Lem and me standing here. The others had gone to spread the word. Been a long time since we've had any decent news like that."

Pap said, "I figure the Scraggs had to be involved in this some way."

"I wouldn't put it past any of the Scraggs," Ed said.

"But if you guys said anything about it on the police radio, old Batim would have heard. He got himself a police scanner last year. Anymore, we get most of our police news through Batim."

"It was Buck, I bet anything," Pap said. "Probably blabbing everything over the radio."

"Doesn't rule out the Scraggs being involved in this thing," Tully said.

"It sure doesn't," Ed agreed.

Tully said, "You hear anything, Ed, anything that might give us a lead into this mess, call my cell phone."

"Sure. Hey, how come you brought Pap along?"

"Not for his social amenities, that's for sure," Tully said. "Mostly, he knows quite a bit about Scraggs and murder."

"Yep," Pap agreed. "I got to admit, though, that this trip has pretty much satiated my appetite for both."

"Mine, too," Tully said. "I've got my Crime Scene Investigation Unit headed up here. A state patrolman's guarding the site now. How long before the whole town knows that, Ed?"

"Take about an hour. We do what we can with limited resources."

Tully and Pap went out and got in the Explorer.

Pap rolled and lit another cigarette. Tully didn't complain. It wouldn't do him any good, anyway. The Explorer's ashtray was already full.

The old man said, "You know that orange fluorescent tape at the opening to the mining road? Well, whoever put that up was probably directing the boys in the Jeep into the ambush."

"You may be right," Tully said. "Otherwise it would be hard to spot that road entrance in the dark."

"There might be a useful fingerprint on that tape," Pap said.

"We should have cut it down. Thanks for telling me now."

That's why he had brought the old man along. Tully couldn't believe his own stupidity, except he had been a bit overloaded. He braked hard, made a bootlegger's turn on the highway, and headed back through Famine toward the old mine road. Details! he thought. I hate the details.

The radio squawked. It was Florence, the 911 operator, back at the office. "We got the local press here demanding we tell it what's going on."

He pressed the talk button. "Copy, Florence. Thanks. Put Barney on."

Barney's voice came over the radio.

"Hi, Bo!"

"Hi, Barney. What do you need to know?"

"We heard you had a murder up there at Famine. Eliot won't tell me anything."

"That's what Eliot is supposed to do, not tell you anything. We had three murders in fact. But I can't tell you much over the radio. Give me your cell phone number and I'll call you later."

Barney gave him the cell phone number.

Tully pulled out his cell phone and called Buck on his.

"You and Susan out at the mining road yet?"

"Just got here."

"You see a little orange fluorescent ribbon right by the road entrance?"

"No."

"It's off to the left and up pretty high, about six inches long."

"Not there, boss."

"Okay, thanks, Buck."

"Just thought I'd mention the tape," Pap said, puffing his skinny little cigarette out the corner of his mouth. "You want me to mention something else?"

Tully nodded, a brief, irritable dip of his head.

"The ambushers had to have some kind of transportation. It's possible they came in over the mountain and walked in from the other side of the berm. But if they're locals, I don't think they like walking that much. I bet there's a trail back in the woods someplace and they rode ATVs in there, three- or four-wheelers."

"Possible," Tully said.

"You probably noticed there wasn't any blood on the trail where they drug out the guy that got hit on the left side of the car. I think they must have rolled him up in a tarp or something. Otherwise there would have been a blood trail. They probably drug him over to the ATVs and hauled him out on one of those. It's not the easiest thing in the world to haul a dead deer on one of those contraptions, and it's even harder to haul a dead man. I suspect some blood may have leaked out on the machine and probably on the trail, too."

"Find the trail and the machine and we'll check it out," Tully said.

"Never can tell," the old man said.

Two state patrolmen were standing next to their cars, which they had used to block the entrance to the road. They were talking to Buck. Susan was sitting in the Suburban.

Tully said to the patrolmen, "You guys see anybody come by and take a piece of fluorescent tape off that tree over there?"

"Matter of fact we did," said one of the patrolmen. "An old guy in bib overalls. Had on one of those earflap caps. Probably lives in Famine. Said he'd marked the road because he'd killed a deer back in there. I'd recognize him if I saw him again."

"Deer season doesn't open until next week," Pap said.

"I suppose," the officer said. "But folks get confused."

Tully nodded. About half the population of Famine was old and wore bib overalls. He wasn't sure about earflap caps. He turned to Pap. "You and Buck drive back in the Explorer. Take Susan with you. Lurch should be along pretty quick, too. You might see if you can find that ATV trail while you're waiting."

"Where you going?"

"To see Vern Littlefield. Not much happens in this part of Blight County he doesn't know about."

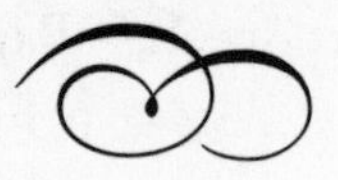

Chapter 11

The half-mile-long driveway from the highway into the Littlefield ranch house was heavily graveled but smooth as a dance floor.

A Super Cub plane was parked in front of a hangar a short ways from the house. Tully could see the nose of a two-engine plane through the open hangar door. The asphalted landing strip stretched away from the hangar and diminished across a hayfield larger than most of the other ranches in the area. A young woman came out onto the porch of the ranch house and watched as Tully walked up.

"You Mrs. Littlefield?" Tully asked.

"I am. Call me Cindy, please. You have to be Sheriff Bo Tully."

"I am. I heard that old dog Littlefield got married again, but nobody told me he had married a teenager."

"Thirty-four hard years actually. But I appreciate the compliment." She laughed. Her voice was husky and incongruous with her youthful appearance. Now that he was closer, he noticed a tiny scar above the upper lip on the left side of her mouth.

Something he found somewhat sexy was that she was able to move her breasts beneath her white, short-sleeved blouse. He tried not to stare but had never before witnessed anything quite like this. He wondered if possibly Littlefield had found her in a circus sideshow. Suddenly a tiny, furry head poked out of the sleeve of her blouse. Tully jumped.

"I guess you've never seen a ferret before, Sheriff."

"Never crawling around inside a woman's blouse, I haven't," Tully said, embarrassed. "I thought maybe you had an unusual talent."

Cindy laughed. "No, just a ferret. His name's Oscar."

"So how long have you and Vern been married?"

"About eight months. Nearly eight. I suppose you're here to talk to Vern. Unfortunately, he went elk hunting. I know, I know, he's got six hundred head of cattle driving him to the poorhouse and he goes after an elk. Maybe he can't even stand the sight of beef anymore. Took off sometime yesterday and drove up to his hunting camp. Told Mitchell he'd be back when he got an elk. He's going to be disappointed he missed you. And the murders!"

"Mitchell?" Tully said. "That's your ranch foreman, right?"

"Sort of."

"You already know about the murders?"

"Not much happens in Famine we don't get to hear about. So when you have three murders in one night, word gets around pretty fast. Come on in, Bo, and rest a bit. You look a little weary."

Tully ran his fingers back through his hair to smooth it and said that he didn't mind if he did. The living room was large, with a massive river-stone fireplace dominating one wall. Three-foot-long log sections were stacked alongside, presumably for fuel. The walls were covered with art. In a prominent place above a leather couch was one of Tully's own paintings.

"I assume you're the same Bo Tully who does the watercolors," Cindy said.

"I am he. Oils, too, when I have the time."

"Vern and I bought that picture from a gallery the last time we were in Los Angeles. It cost an arm and a leg. Vern's, of course. He moaned for days afterwards."

Tully smiled modestly. The gallery had somehow neglected to inform him of the sale. He supposed his share of the money was slowly making its way in his direction. He sat down on the couch, its creamy tan leather seeming to envelop him.

"Can I get you something to drink?" Cindy asked.

"Some water would be great."

Cindy left and returned with a glass of water with ice cubes.

"Thanks, I really needed this," Tully said. He drank. "So what's this I hear about Vern giving up the cattle business?"

"He's actually doing it. Various meatpacking companies have been coming in and loading up cows. He must be serious. He says he's lost money on cows the last five years. 'You have an enemy, give him a cow. He'll soon be bankrupt.' Vern tells that joke to everyone he meets."

Tully sipped his water. "He fire his cowhands?" he said.

"He's going to, he says. He feels bad about that, too. They've been with him a long time."

Tully saw out the front window a Blight City ambulance going by out on the highway, probably to pick up the last two bodies.

"It's done," he said. "Driving into Famine this morning, I met Vern's four ranch hands. They said they'd been fired by Vern's foreman."

"Why, that's strange. I know Vern intended to do it himself. He was dreading it."

"Not like Vern to take the easy way out," Tully said.

"No, it isn't."

"Any chance I can meet the foreman?"

"Sure. His name is Robert Mitchell. I haven't seen him or the other one around today. They stay at the next house down from here. Vern's parents used to live there. They're even getting their own cook. She's supposed to show up any day."

"The other one?"

"Yes, Harry Kincaid."

Tully took out a notebook and wrote down the names.

"Vern seems to take pretty good care of Mitchell and Kincaid. I suppose they're the ones who'll be in charge of the grapes."

"Grapes?"

"I understood from the old crew that Vern was kicking out the cows and turning the ranch into a vineyard."

"Vern doesn't discuss his plans much with me," she said. "But I'd like grapes a whole lot better than I like cows."

"Me, too," Tully said. "Anyway, I'll stop back and see if I can talk to Mitchell and Kincaid."

"Come by anytime," Cindy said.

"Thanks. Oh, one more thing. My father and I and one of my deputies will be staying up here tonight. I was wondering if we could sleep in your hotel. We have sleeping bags with us."

"I guess that would be all right. There are some old army cots in some of the rooms."

"Great," Tully said. "I appreciate it. By the way, if you hear from Vern, please give me a call."

"I certainly will. Right now, though, our phones are out. The phone company should be showing up anytime to fix them."

"Good luck," Tully said. "Well, I'd better get back to the Last Hope Road. We've got a real mess out there."

"The Last Hope," Cindy said. "The Last Hope Canyon is where Vern has his dam. I didn't know that was where those men were killed."

"Vern has his dam up there?" Tully said.

"Yes, it's about a mile up the canyon. He and his dad built it about thirty years ago, during an energy shortage. He sells the electricity to Central Electric."

"Have you seen it?"

"Vern and I drove up to it once. We drove over the mountain and down the Last Hope Canyon. The dam is all automatic. Vern monitors it from here. He's got all the gauges and everything in the basement. If something goes wrong at the dam or someone breaks into the enclosure, an alarm goes off here. The alarm has never gone off, at least not since I've been here."

"You think Vern would mind if I walked in from the bottom of the canyon and took a look at his dam?"

"I'm sure he wouldn't. I hope you don't think the dam had anything to do with the murders."

Tully laughed. "No, not at all. I just think it's pretty neat, having your own private dam. If I'm ever able to get out of law enforcement, I might build one of my own."

"Vern says it's a whole lot less trouble than cows."

"I'll bet it is," Tully said. He nodded at the wood stacked by the fireplace. "Vern cut his own firewood?"

"Yes, how else would you ever find logs like that? I can't even lift them. But the fireplace is so big, it seems to require logs."

On his way out to the Explorer, Tully saw a green pickup truck coming in the driveway. He leaned against his front fender and waited. Two men were in the cab. The truck pulled up across from the Explorer. The light bar and the Sheriff's Department emblem on the Explorer did not appear to please the occupants.

"Howdy," Tully said. He moseyed over to the open window of the driver. "You must be the fellas who work for Vern. I'm Sheriff Bo Tully."

"Any problem, Sheriff?" the driver said, frowning, not at all friendly.

"No, none at all, not counting I got three people murdered up north of Famine. Fact is, I just stopped by to visit with Vern, but I hear he's gone off on an elk hunt."

The men in the truck seemed to relax. The driver reached out and shook hands with Tully. "I'm Robert Mitchell, Vern's foreman. This is Harry Kincaid, my number one guy." Kincaid stared straight at Tully, his expression unchanging.

"Nice to meet you," Tully said. "I was just wondering, did Vern ever mention to you when he intended to return from his hunt?"

"Not me," Mitchell said.

Kincaid continued to stare.

"I guess maybe when he gets an elk," Mitchell said.

"Thanks anyway," Tully said. "Good meeting you fellas."

Tully glanced back at the house. Cindy Littlefield was standing in the window watching. She did not look happy.

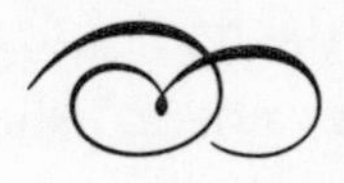

Chapter 12

When Tully got back to the Last Hope Road, one of the state troopers had left. He told the other one he could leave, too, that the situation was just about cleaned up. He drove the Explorer under the crime-scene tape, through the creek and down the road to the clearing. A Blight City ambulance was backed up to the Jeep. He pulled the Explorer over into the brush so that the ambulance could get by. The bodies were still in the same position as when he had left. The ambulance driver and his assistant were out of their vehicle, both of them smoking cigarettes. He wondered vaguely how much they paid ambulance personnel these days, that they could afford to smoke. Susan walked out around the Jeep, blowing some strands of hair out of her face. She was stripping off a pair of bloody latex gloves.

"I called in the ambulance," she said. "I'd like to get the bodies back to the morgue as soon as possible."

"That's fine," he said. "My Crime Scene Investigation Unit is on its way, but he won't need the bodies."

"I discovered Pap's pretty good with a camera," she said. "He's photographed everything, including the spots back in the trees where the ambushers waited. They had some heavy firepower, automatics of some kind."

"Automatics don't seem like something our local boys would have lying around."

"Hard to tell what boys have lying around these days," she said. "I went through the victims' pockets and billfolds. They both have L.A. addresses and lots of cash. The two in the front seat both had guns still in their holsters. Holt, the chap over the fence, probably had a gun, too, but we can't find it. He didn't have a holster, not one we've found, anyway."

Tully walked around the car and back to Susan. "The thing I can't figure is how the guy on the fence made it out of the back seat. The two shooters in the trees could have sprayed the whole length of the car with automatic weapons fire in a couple of seconds."

"The back seat was riddled with bullets, too," Susan said.

"Right. And so Holt should have been killed right here at the car. How did he avoid getting hit in the car?"

"I see what you mean," Susan said. "The back seat area is shot to pieces. It doesn't look as if anyone could have survived that."

Susan walked over and started talking to the ambulance guys. Pap came out of the woods.

"I was right," the old man said. "As usual."

"How so?" Tully asked.

"There's an old skid trail back in there a hundred yards or so. The shooters drove some ATVs in on it and parked them there. Then they walked through the woods and set up the ambush."

"Were you able to tell how many?"

"Kind of. There were three pretty good-size ATVs, all of them four-wheelers. Each of them could carry two people if they were on pretty good terms with each other, so there couldn't have been more than six people all together, maybe as few as three."

"Shoe tracks?"

"None I could find," Pap said. "Looked like they drug something around to erase any tracks. I walked down the trail a ways and picked up the tracks of the ATVs."

"Folks drive ATVs all over this country," Tully said. "Could be anybody riding them around here."

"Except for one thing," Pap said, taking out the makings from his jacket pocket. He carefully rolled himself a cigarette.

"And that thing is?" Tully said irritably.

"I found a splash of blood."

"And what did you conclude from that?"

"If the fence guy did in fact shoot one of the ambushers or someone else standing back in the woods, as we think he did, they would have had to wrap the dead guy up in a poncho or a tarp or something to keep him from leaving a bloody trail all the way over to the ATVs. They've got the dead guy tied onto one of the ATVs, and as they're riding out the tarp slips and spills some blood. The other shooters stop and try to cover the blood with dirt, but it's dark and they don't do a good job. So you can see the blood is on top of the track they came in on and that one of the ATVs went over some of it on the way out. So we can be pretty sure it ain't blood from a deer or something."

"Maybe it wasn't a mistake bringing you along," Tully said.

"Well, I'm enjoying my birthday."

Susan came over with the ambulance driver. "If we're finished with the bodies, the guys can get them to the morgue."

"If you're done with them."

"I've done everything I can here. I'm going to head in, too. See if I can get the autopsies started."

Tully didn't like the image of this beautiful woman performing autopsies. "Where's Buck?" he said.

"I've got him out looking for the gun you think Holt may have dropped or thrown away."

The ambulance attendants were loading one of the bodies onto a stretcher.

"I'll call the office and get someone to send a tow truck out and we'll get this car impounded where we can check it out."

"Good idea," Susan said, walking over to him. "You know, this would be a really nice spot in the woods if it didn't have blood all over it."

The ambulance pulled out.

"It's getting better already," Tully said. "Speaking of blood, Pap found a patch of it over on a skid trail the ambushers apparently drove their ATVs in on. It's almost sure to be human, but would you check it for us?

See if it's at least the same type as the blood over in the woods. Later we'll see if the state crime lab can match the DNA."

"Sure. Then I'll probably take off. See you back in town."

"Yes, you will," Tully said.

She gave him her nice smile. Probably already in love with me, Tully thought.

Buck walked back into the clearing. Tully asked him if he had found anything. Buck shook his head. "Getting on toward supper," he said. "You mind if I head back in?"

"Yes, I mind," Tully said. "I need you here. Go get some coffee if you want."

Buck seemed pleased. It was nice to be needed.

Tully said to Susan, "Now that we've got the bodies out of here, I'm going over the berm and walk up the road to see if I can find anything that might bring our dead friends out here for the little ambush. You want to go along?"

Susan thought for a moment, massaging her lower back with her hands. "Sure. Let me do that patch of blood Pap found, and I'll be ready to go. By the way, I'm pretty sure the victims in the car died at three thirty-eight this morning."

"Wow, three thirty-eight. Your science is that accurate now?"

"No. One of the bullets hit the driver's watch. Stopped it at three thirty-eight."

Chapter 13

Tully and Susan climbed over the berm and started up the road. "So Pap was right," he said. "That was human blood."

"He was right. I bet he was fun to grow up with."

Tully glanced at her to see if she was kidding. She apparently wasn't. "Oh yeah, he was a delight," he said.

"You mean he wasn't?"

"I never even knew he was my father until I was about ten. All I knew, he was the sheriff and just about everybody in town was afraid of him. We kids in particular. 'You eat those Brussels sprouts or I'll call the sheriff,' parents would say. Those Brussels sprouts would vanish as if by magic."

"Good heavens, he doesn't seem like the kind of man anyone would be afraid of."

"I guess that's part of his MO."

"Are you the kind of sheriff people are afraid of?"

Tully kicked a rock up the road. "Me? Naw, I'm a pussycat."

"I bet."

The road was steep and winding, and Tully paused often to look around at the scenery. Each pause caused him to take a little longer to catch his breath. Susan seemed unbothered by the climb. Probably a jogger, Tully thought. Just his luck. "Hey, huckleberry brush!" he exclaimed on the third switchback. He would have to remember this for the following summer.

They came to a tiny spring running out of the bank above the road.

"You want a drink?" Tully said, dipping a finger in the stream. "It's ice-cold water."

"You've got to be kidding! Don't tell me you would actually drink from that! You could get giardiasis!"

"Giardiasis? Around here we call that beaver fever."

"Why am I not surprised?"

"Of course I'm kidding about taking a drink from this. Sure, maybe if I was dying of thirst." Tully was dying of thirst. "By the way, the road is kind of muddy here. Like me to carry you across?"

"Somebody else has waded across, I think I probably can, too. The mud is about half an inch deep!"

"Thought it was worth a try," Tully said.

Susan laughed.

Off in the distance, they could see the Blight River meandering along between its borders of cottonwoods. Several small lakes were visible in the distance. They could see the town of Famine, a cluster of miniature buildings neatly arranged along tiny streets. Famine looked a lot better from a distance than it did up close. Susan, on the other hand, looked pretty darn good up close. He was pretty sure she would look even better the closer he got.

"It's so beautiful," she said, peering out at the valley.

"Yeah, Idaho is a beautiful state. But Blight County itself is a corrupt little place."

"Corrupt?"

"Only in the good sense. Most of the politicians can be bought, but they don't charge much. Even the poor can afford a politician or two. It's very democratic that way."

They came to a road cut into the canyon wall. It led down to Vern Littlefield's dam. The reservoir behind the dam stretched back up the canyon and around a bend. A high, padlocked gate prevented them from walking down the road. The dam and an adjacent building were enclosed by a Cyclone fence with coils of razor wire along the top.

"Vern apparently maintains his dam by driving over the mountain between here and the ranch," Tully said. "According to his wife, Cindy, he's got a security system that lets him know if anybody is fooling around the dam."

"It's a pretty modest little dam," Susan said.

"Yeah, but I've always wanted my own little dam."

Susan smiled.

Rounding a craggy corner, they came to the Last Hope Mine. It had been a much larger operation than Tully had imagined. Tailings from the mine filled the entire upper half of a gully and had been bulldozed flat on top. Most of the buildings, roofed with rusted corrugated steel, were still intact. A large, open, timber-framed structure held several huge tubs that Tully thought probably had contained acid baths to separate the gold from rock. A dozen small cabins were situated in a flat area that had been dozed out of the mountainside, residences, apparently, for the workers and their families.

"The Last Hope was quite a mine," Tully said. "I didn't expect anything like this."

"Anything in particular you're looking for?" Susan said.

"Maybe it's just that I've always wanted my own little gold mine."

"With your own little dam and your own little gold mine you'd be all set," Susan said, clearly trying not to laugh.

"That's about the way I figure it," Tully said.

"What exactly do you have in mind for your gold mine?"

"Oh, something small enough that I could work it myself. I saw this bit on television once about an old guy, he must have been ninety-something, and he had this vein of gold he worked with just a pick. He'd whack out a few rocks and put them in a sack and carry them back to his cabin. He'd built this rock crusher out of some pipe and other stuff and he'd pound the rock down into a powder and then take his gold pan and wash out the gold. I said to myself, 'Perfect!'"

"It doesn't sound like a great life to me, living up in

the mountains all alone and pounding rocks all day."

"I was afraid of that," Tully said. He and Susan walked over to the mine entrance. The explosion that closed it had brought down tons of rock. A few timbers protruded from the pile of rubble.

"Nobody's going to get in there," Tully said. "Unfortunately, the owners of a lot of mines in these mountains simply walked off and left them. Some kids found one a few years ago that still had boxes of old dynamite stacked inside. It was so old the sticks were sweating nitroglycerin. The kids had twenty-two-caliber rifles with them, and if they had fired one shot into that stack of dynamite, we'd have been lucky to find so much as a hair from any one of them. Somehow, one of them must have had a lick of sense, and they ended up reporting the mine back to us. We blew it up. It was quite a bit of fun, actually, but the blast shook practically every window in the county."

Susan shook her head, whether it was in disbelief or simple amusement Tully couldn't tell.

"I imagine the miners who lived in these cabins had a pretty rough time of it," Tully said. "Particularly in the winter."

"They had a terrific view, though."

"It's nice," Tully said.

"We'd better head back," Susan said. "You probably want those autopsies done tonight."

Tully still didn't like the image that popped into his head of Susan doing autopsies. It ruined some of his other images. "If you could just do the fence guy tonight, that would be great. We know the victims in the car were killed with automatic weapons, probably Uzis or Mac 10s."

"I'll at least do Mr. Holt," Susan said. "How about you? What are you going to do?"

"I think we'll stay up here. I was planning on camping out, but it's gotten so cold it might even snow. I asked Mrs. Littlefield if it would be all right if we stayed in the old hotel. She said there are some old army cots in there."

"That old hotel looks haunted," Susan said. "I saw it on the way up here. Your secretary told me to watch for it."

"Haunted? Maybe I'll check with Ed at the service station. There might be a B and B in Famine."

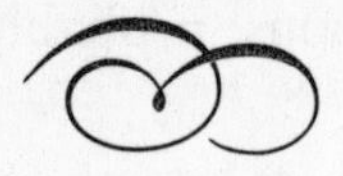

Chapter 14

Pap was sitting on a log next to the road, blowing into his cupped hands to warm them. Lurch was poking dowels into the Jeep's bullet holes. A wrecker and its driver waited for the vehicle.

"I thought you'd taken off for good with Susan," Pap said. "I knew I should have warned her about you."

"You're a good one to be warning anybody," Tully said.

"He was a perfect gentleman at all times," Susan said.

"He was? Obviously, I didn't raise him right."

"Or at all," Tully said.

"That, too," Pap said.

Tully pointed at Lurch. "This is Lurch, my Crime Scene Investigation Unit," he said. "He also goes by the name of Byron Proctor."

Lurch nodded at Susan.

She smiled and said, "Hi, Byron."

Tully knew his Crime Scene Investigation Unit had to come as a shock to anyone seeing it for the first time. But Susan seemed to take it in stride.

"We going to head back to Blight or spend the night here?" Pap asked.

"I'd thought we might camp out. But it has turned pretty cold. I asked Mrs. Littlefield if we can sack out in the old hotel. She said sure."

"The hotel? It's probably haunted," Pap said.

"If you believe all the stories, half the places in Blight County are haunted. You're certainly welcome to stay with us, Susan."

"In a haunted hotel? You're just trying to make me think a night of autopsies is a pretty great thing. No, I've got to head back."

"I brought along some homemade elk sausages to roast over a campfire," Pap said. "Some fried potatoes and onions, too, and fresh rolls. Baked them myself."

"You're starting to make that haunted hotel sound pretty good," Susan said. "But no, sorry, I've got to get back. It's been nice hanging out with both of you. See you back in Blight City."

She got in her Suburban and left.

Tully squatted down next to his CSI unit. "Figure out anything yet, Lurch?"

"Yup," Lurch said. "It's kind of odd. You see these bullet holes in the front door. The dowels in them all converge out toward where one shooter was standing. He shot up only the front seat instead of spraying the whole car."

"I see that."

"The other shooter, he sprayed bullets only into the back seat."

"That's weird," Tully said. "Why didn't both of them just spray the whole car and be done with it?"

"Don't know. But look at this. Most of the dowels in the rear door seem to slant to a shooter who's standing back in the woods but to the rear of the car. Pap didn't find any signs somebody was standing over there, though. No ferns trampled down or anything."

"I'm not going to guess, Lurch," Tully said. "Tell me."

Lurch stood up and opened the door. The dowels now pointed to where the second gunman had stood.

"The door was open!" Tully said.

"Right. Somebody must have shut it after the shooting stopped."

"But why would it be open?" Tully wondered aloud. "If somebody was sitting in the right rear seat and jumped out, he would have been an easy target. But there's no blood on the ground or in the rear seat."

"I think you're on to something," Pap said.

"Let's suppose the first shooter starts to spray the front seat," Tully said, tugging on the corner of his mustache. "The second gunman holds back to let the person in the right rear seat open the door and dive out of the way. That gives Holt just enough time to go out the left rear door, before the second shooter sprays the rear seat. Holt's got a gun out and is firing in all directions. By chance he hits someone standing back in the woods, maybe another potential shooter."

"So why does the second shooter let the guy in the right rear seat get away?" Lurch said.

"Because the guy in the right rear seat set up the ambush," Tully said.

Chapter 15

The wrecker driver hooked up the car and left. Tully and Pap got in the Explorer and started to drive to the entrance of the mine road. Suddenly Tully stopped, got out and walked back to Byron. "It's getting kind of dark, Lurch. You got a flash on that camera of yours?"

"Sure."

"I've got one more thing I'd like you to do before you head in. There's a tiny spring a couple hundred yards up the road and the ground is wet there. There are a couple of shoe prints in the mud. One is going uphill and the other down. I didn't think much about them until now, but I think each set was made by different people, one going uphill and the other down. You'll be able to figure out Susan's and my prints, because they'll be a lot fresher. What I want to know is if those other prints were made by different people. I'm pretty sure they were. If you've got some of that dental-stone powder, make a couple casts. Might turn out to be something."

"You got it, boss."

"I want you to do some tests on the car tomorrow."

"Gee, Sheriff, I was hoping to have tomorrow off."

"I guess that's okay. What's happening, a big date?" Tully almost laughed at the absurdity.

"Yeah, I haven't seen my girlfriend all week."

Tully stared at him, astonished. "You have a girlfriend?"

"Sure. I got her picture right here." Lurch dug out his billfold, took out the photo and handed it to him.

Tully stared at it. "Good gosh! She's beautiful, Lurch!"

"Yeah. She's really smart, too. She's a cytogeneticist at a Boise hospital."

"A cyto—what?"

"A cytogeneticist. She studies chromosomes."

Tully felt dazed. Lurch? "A girlfriend," he said.

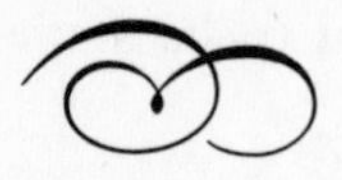

Chapter 16

At the entrance to the Last Hope Road, Pap asked, "You want to leave the crime-scene tape up?"

"I don't know," Tully said. "What do you think?"

"Won't do much good around here. People want to look, they will, tape or not. Probably just attract attention."

"That's what I figure," Tully said. He got out and stripped down all the tape. When he got back in, Pap said, "You got a heater in this thing? I'm about half froze."

"Good heater. In ten minutes, you'll be warm as toast."

"By then I'll be dead."

"Better not be. I've had about all of that I can stand for one day."

Fifteen minutes later, they were driving through Famine. "You want to eat here?" Tully asked.

"No," the old man said. "I told you, I brought along some good elk sausages."

"I just thought you might be too tired to cook."

"Never too tired to cook elk sausages."

Tully pulled out his cell phone and dialed. "Hello, Buck? Yeah, Tully here. Meet us at the old hotel on the Littlefield ranch. You and Pap and I are spending the night there. . . . I don't care if it is haunted. You're staying there with us!" He hung up.

Pap chuckled. "Wish all I had to worry about was ghosts."

It was nearly dark when they reached the hotel. Tully could still make out among the dried-up weeds the stone foundations of the houses and other buildings that had been burned down. The hotel had been set off from the other houses, at the foot of a hill occupied by the town's cemetery.

Pap got a small propane lantern out of his pack, lit it and hung it from a nail on the hotel's porch. Tully left the Explorer's lights shining down what once had been the town's only street. He walked around in the light gathering scraps of boards for the campfire. When he had an armful, he hauled them back in front of the porch and dumped them. Pap, who had been exploring the inside of the hotel, hauled out three chairs.

"It ain't too bad," he informed Tully. "Dusty but sure a lot warmer than out here."

"It'll be warmer out here, too, as soon as I get this fire going," Tully said. "You got any paper on you?"

"Paper, ha. I got this." Pap unwrapped aluminum foil from around what at first appeared to be a large candy bar. "Fire starter," he said. "Never go out in the wilds without your fire starter. Been many a man froze to death for not having the foresight to take along his fire starter. Let this be a lesson to you, Bo."

"Give it here."

Pap tossed him the stick. Tully stuck it under some of the smaller boards he had broken up and held a lighted match to it. As Tully said later, a person could have welded with that fire starter. Underwater.

"You make this fire starter yourself?" he asked the old man.

"Yeah. You want the recipe?"

"Maybe, but I'll wait until after my mustache and eyebrows grow back."

The lights of Buck's Explorer came down the highway and turned off toward the hotel. He pulled up next to the other Explorer.

"I don't like the idea of staying in this old hotel," he told Tully as he walked up and held his hands over the fire. He glanced at Pap, who was squatted down cutting potatoes and onions into a large black skillet.

"Drive to Blight City if you want to," Tully replied, "but I've got to have you back up here at six in the morning. We have a lot of people to talk to, and I personally don't want to stay up here any longer than I have to."

Buck watched Pap open a folding grill next to the fire and rake coals under it with a broken branch. "Whatcha cooking there, Pap?"

"Grilling some elk sausages, along with some fried potatoes and onions. Got some good rolls, too. Baked them myself."

"What's for dessert?"

"Whiskey. Brought along a fifth of Cabin Still."

"I guess maybe I can stay at the hotel," Buck said. "It's just that you hear about this place being haunted enough times, it makes you wonder."

"Buck, you ever hear of a ghost actually hurting somebody?" Pap asked.

"No."

"Well, there you go."

"Just seeing a ghost would be more than enough hurt as far as I'm concerned," Buck said. "But I'm staying. You might just as well throw a couple of those sausages on for me, Pap."

"I already did."

After supper, which Tully thought was about as good as any he had ever eaten, the three of them sat around the fire and talked. Buck and Pap smoked cigars Pap had brought, and Tully joined them in drinking whiskey out of paper cups. Pap had always had a talent for living well. Tully was tired and had seen more than enough death for one day, but this was one of the better evenings he'd had in a long while.

He held up his cup of whiskey. "Happy birthday, Pap!"

"Your birthday, hunh?" Buck said. "Happy birthday, Pap."

"Thanks, I guess. Bo give me these here murders as a present. All I can say is, you shouldn't have, Bo, you shouldn't have."

Tully laughed. "I didn't expect it to be quite this big of a present."

"You got any idea who done 'em, Bo?" Buck asked.

"No. How about you, Pap?"

"I figure it has to have something to do with drugs, all the cash in their pockets, the L.A. guys."

"You're probably right," Tully said. "Seems like just about everything that happens nowadays has something to do with drugs. It's pretty clear the dead guys were set up. For some reason, they got themselves lured onto an old mining road."

"I kind of like your idea about there being a fourth guy in the car," Pap said. "I think you're right about a fourth guy setting them up. Otherwise, there's no reason the shooters didn't spray the whole car with automatic fire. Holt could never have got out of the car otherwise."

"That's about the way I see it," Tully said. "If that's right, we've got two ambushers in the trees on the right side of the car, two guys killed in the car, another guy in the car who set the other guys up and who went out the right rear door. Then there's a fourth guy back in the woods, somebody that the Holt fellow probably killed by chance."

"Sounds about right to me," Pap said. "As far as I could tell, there were only three four-wheel ATVs used by the ambushers to come and go on. That would be enough. It was probably one of the shooters at the Jeep who tracked Holt down and killed him. So that probably means one ATV was left behind for him. The guy in the car who lured the others in probably drove out on one ATV. One of the shooters drove the other ATV out with the dead guy strapped on behind."

Buck shook his head. "Sounds to me like you fellas got this whole mess figured out."

"Not quite," Tully said.

After Pap and Tully had told a few ghost stories to get Buck in the proper mood to spend a night in a haunted hotel, they decided to turn in. Tully gave each of them a sleeping bag and kept one for himself. He told Buck to park both vehicles in a shed next to the hotel and close the doors.

"No point in advertising that we're staying here," he said. "Pour some water on the fire and kick dirt over it too, Buck."

The three of them each selected a room on the second floor.

"Wait a minute," Buck said. "Maybe we all should sleep in the same room."

"Why is that?" Pap said.

"It might be warmer," Buck said.

"Not warm enough that I want to listen to you snore all night," Tully said.

"It was just a suggestion."

Tully went into his room. Moonlight poured through the window. The only furnishing was an old army cot, but at least it was dry and inside. He rolled out his sleeping bag on the cot. He hung his coat on the doorknob and removed his boots and belt. He took off his wristwatch and put it on top of his boots, so that he could read it when he woke up at night. If he woke up. He doubted if he would wake up before morning, though, because it had been a long while since he had felt this tired. Finally, he stood up his flashlight next to his boots and placed his Colt Woodsman next to the flashlight.

About one-thirty in the morning, something awoke him. He glanced at his watch. It said 1:30 but he read it upside down and thought it said 7:00. The moonlight was still pouring in the window. Outside it was bright as day, and he thought it was morning. Then he heard someone moving in the hallway. He thought it was probably Pap or Buck, but to be on the safe side he stuck the Colt Woodsman in the waistband at the back of his pants. He opened the door and stepped out. A tall, slender figure was standing right in front of him. Tully blurted out, "Up against the wall!" Thinking about it later, he remembered that he might also have blurted out a twelve-letter obscenity very much against department policy. Fortunately, the figure was startled even worse than Tully. It turned and, without being told, spread its hands up against the wall, apparently having had previous experience in assuming the position. Tully reached back for the Colt. It was gone! He had sucked in his gut at the moment of seeing the figure and the Colt had slipped down into the crotch of his boxer shorts. He had forgotten all about the diet and the lost twenty pounds. "Don't look back!" he told the figure. He then unzipped the fly of his pants and reached in to get hold of the gun. He worried about touching the trigger and hoped he had left the safety on. At that moment the person looked back. He shouted out his own twelve-letter obscenity, turned and ran down the stairs.

Just then Buck burst into the hallway carrying his boots. "Are they in the hotel yet?" he croaked.

"I just saw one of them," Tully said, finally getting hold of his gun.

"Oh no," Buck moaned. "The rest must already be downstairs then."

"What?" Tully yelled. "You saw them!"

"Yes! I looked out the window and I saw all of them streaming down from the graveyard! They're wearing these old-time clothes. I figure they must be the dead townsfolk! When they got to town they'd see all their houses had been burned down. Then they'd head for the only place left, the hotel!"

"You were dreaming!" Tully shouted. "This guy was no ghost! Ghosts don't make any sound when they run."

"If those folks are downstairs, I'll make a sound when I run. And if it wasn't a ghost, how come you didn't shoot?"

"Because I don't just shoot people if I can help it!"

"Pap would have shot him!"

"You bet," Pap said. He had stepped out into the hallway, a pistol in his hand.

"Figures," Tully said.

"I don't care what you say," Buck said, "I'm sleeping in your room, Bo!"

"Okay," Tully said. He didn't even care if Buck snored. "Just don't dream anymore. I don't want to hear about your dreams."

"It wasn't a dream," Buck said. "I saw them, streaming down through all that moonlit grass and . . ."

"Shut up!" Tully said.

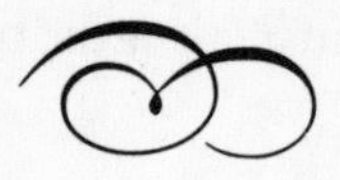

Chapter 17

"It wasn't a dream," Buck told Pap. "I seen them clear as day, all these folks trooping down off the cemetery hill."

The three of them were seated at a booth in Dave's House of Fry. They were eating giant pancakes with bacon and eggs on the side.

"It was a dream," Tully said, "and I don't want to hear any more about it."

Deedee and Carol, the two waitresses, were both making over Pap. He was slurping it up. Tully wasn't sure if either he or Buck had gone back to sleep after the incident with the intruder. In his case, it certainly didn't feel like it, but Pap seemed well rested. He wished he could sleep as soundly as the old man. "You got any idea who the guy in the hotel was last night?" Pap said to Tully.

"No, I wish I did. If I had to guess, I'd say it was Lem Scragg. But I never got a good look at his face. He obviously was after something."

"Maybe he was a ghost," Pap said, shoveling a forkful of scrambled eggs into his mouth.

"That's what I think!" said Buck.

"Shut up, both of you," Tully said. "I don't want to hear anything more about ghosts. By the way, Pap, where'd you have the gun hidden? In your pack?"

"Course not," Pap said. "Had it in the cooler."

"So, what do you want me to do today?" Buck asked.

"Well, I figure those guys in the car didn't stay here in Famine, because there's no place for them to stay. And maybe they didn't want to be seen about town, anyway. What's the nearest place up north they could have stayed?"

"Cedar Hill Lodge is still open for the season," Buck said. "They got cabins and a few hunters stay there this time of year. It's about twenty-five miles north of the mining road."

"What makes you think they stayed anywhere?" Pap said. "Susan fixed the time of death at three thirty-eight. They rented the car at ten o'clock at night in Spokane. That's four and a half hours. It takes about four hours for them to drive down here from Spokane. Why would they need a motel?"

"Yeah," Buck said. "Why would they need a motel? The motel would be closed for the night anyway. There's not even a gas station open between here and Spokane that time of night."

"I don't care, Buck. Drive up there and see if three men in a Jeep rental stopped for the night. If they did, find out which cabins they rented. Get those cabins locked up. Pap and I will check out a few people here, just in case they did come into town."

"Seems like a waste of time," Buck said.

"I suppose, but maybe they did stop and get a cabin," Tully said. "If they hadn't got themselves killed, they would have had to sleep sometime, probably later in the day. Maybe they had to use the bathrooms. What else have we got?"

"Not much," Buck said. "Tell you what, Bo. I'll call Cedar Hill and see if anybody with a Jeep stopped there and rented a cabin in the middle of the night. No point in driving all the way up there if they didn't."

"Okay, call."

After breakfast, Tully and Pap drove into Famine and stopped at Ed's Gas-N-Grub. Ed was out in the garage side of the station fixing a flat tire.

"How's it going?" Ed said, looking up from the rubber plug he had inserted in the tire. He wiped his hands on a dirty cloth hanging from the tire-changing machine.

"Fair to middling," Tully answered. "Thought you might be able to help us out a little, Ed."

"As long as it doesn't involve arithmetic."

"It don't," Pap said.

"Or grammar either," Tully added. "You've probably heard that the car involved in the shooting was a new black Jeep Grand Cherokee."

"I did hear that. If your question is, did I see it or did those folks stop for gas, the answer is no. I'd remember a Grand Cherokee."

"That was my first question. The next is, have you

noticed anybody in or around town suddenly having more money than usual?"

Ed straightened up and moved his shoulders back and forth as if working out a kink. "I wouldn't want them to hear I told you so, but both Lister and Lem Scragg seem to have come into a fair amount of money lately."

"How so?"

"As you probably know, neither of them has ever worked at a regular job in his entire miserable life. But both of them seem to have more money than usual."

Pap was concentrating on rolling a cigarette. "We didn't see signs of a lot of money when we was out there."

"Maybe not. Just thought I'd mention it."

"Is that where Lister and Lem still live, out at Batim's?"

"Yeah," Ed said. "I think they live in those trailers out back, those old mobile homes. They both got wives or girlfriends, change them about as often as their shirts, so I don't know which. There's a whole passel of kids running around there. I think they all feed off Batim, or at least used to."

"What about Batim, how does he make a living?"

"I reckon he steals what he needs. He certainly can't make much off that ranch of his."

Pap lit his skinny little cigarette. "Some of these folks live on air," he said. "There ain't no other way they could possibly survive otherwise. They just keep on going no matter what."

"Seems that way," Ed said. "Oh, they seem better off the last couple of years, don't ask me why."

"One more question," Tully said. "What do you know about the crew out at the Littlefield ranch?"

"Mitchell and Kincaid? Not much. They showed up out of nowhere about four years ago. Yesterday, Littlefield let his old crew go, real cowboys who have worked for him for years. These two obviously don't know much about cattle, but apparently Vern is selling off his herds."

Ed went back to working on the flat. Pap watched him intently, as if he was thinking of taking up tire work. Tully strolled along the garage's steel workbench, looking at Ed's tools. Tully loved tools. I should have been a mechanic, he thought, the work would be so much cleaner. He wandered back over to Ed, who was inflating the tire. "I met what's left of Littlefield's crew last night," he said.

Ed said, "Mitchell seems to be the foreman. He's nice enough, but that Kincaid is a cold son-of-a-gun. Never says a word. He's from around here originally, part of that Kincaid clan back in the hills."

"I doubt either of them ever sat a horse," Tully said.

"They don't have to anymore," Ed said. "Littlefield's got four or five ATVs they can use for driving cattle. The nice thing about an ATV is, you leave it and come back, it's right where you left it. Turn your back for a second and your horse could be in the next county."

Pap and Tully chuckled. Both of them hated horses.

Tully thanked Ed for his time and information and they walked over to the General Store.

"What you want at the store?" Pap asked. "Probably cost twice what it would back in Blight."

"Thought I might pick up a few snacks. Never can tell when we might get back to town."

"You going up the Last Hope Road again? You and Susan already checked the mine out. Of course this time you might be able to keep your mind more on business."

"It was strictly business the last time, you dirty old man. But the fact we didn't find anything doesn't mean there wasn't something there. Maybe I'll have Dave go up and look around."

"Dave the Indian?"

"Yeah, Dave the Indian."

A clean blue Mercury Sable was parked in front of the store. A person didn't see that many new Mercury Sables in Famine, but it was clean and that caught Tully's attention. He walked around the car, looking in the windows, and then he and Pap went into the store.

Tully said "Hi" to the girl at the cash register. She grinned at him. Movie star beautiful. Tully wondered if it was something in the water that made so many of the girls in Famine beautiful. Or maybe it was that it had been six weeks since Gail had bailed out on him. Tully walked over to the magazine and paperback racks. A well-dressed woman of thirty-something was thumbing through a Danielle Steel paperback, apparently to see if she had already read it. She didn't look like a local. She wore a tweed suit over a blue blouse, and her ash-blond hair had been coiffed by an expert, probably someone named Pierre or Maurice. Tully casually unbuttoned his suede jacket so that it revealed the sheriff's badge on his belt.

"Those any good?" he asked.

She glanced at him, took in the badge. "If you like romance," she said.

"Matter of fact, I do," he said. "Haven't read much about it, though. Maybe I should."

"Probably wouldn't hurt," the lady said, and went back to her book.

"That your Sable out front?"

"My what?"

"Your car? A Mercury Sable."

"Oh, right. I hope it isn't illegally parked."

"Shoot, up here you could park in the middle of the road and upside down, and it wouldn't be illegal. It's just that we folks here in Famine don't get a lot of tourists stopping by."

She put the book back on the rack. Tully could tell he was starting to get on her nerves.

"Actually, I'm just passing through. I'm on my way down to Boise for a new job. Anything else on your mind, officer?"

"Nope. Except I guess you probably flew into Spokane International, where you rented the car."

She slowly turned from the racks of books and looked steadily at him. "I guess maybe you're not one of those hick cops on the make that I took you for," she said. "Yes, you got that exactly right. I did fly into Spokane International and rented the car."

"Actually, I am pretty hicky," Tully said, tugging on the corner of his mustache. "So how come you didn't just fly into Boise for your job?"

"I knew you were about to ask that. It's because I wanted to see Idaho, and I'm glad I did. It's beautiful."

"Yep," Tully said. "We got a whole lot of scenery here, more than we need. I'm real sorry to bother you, ma'am, but we've just had this sort of event here, and we kinda got to talk to anybody new that shows up." It was his best imitation of a hick cop.

Her blue-green eyes seemed to freeze in her face. "What kind of event?"

"Oh, nothing a lady like yourself would be interested in."

"Well, I can assure you, I don't know anything about any event in this town. But whatever it was, you're starting to make me very nervous."

"Please don't let me upset you," Tully said, raising his hands as if in surrender. "By the way, I think I'll try one of them Danielle Steels. Maybe it'll teach me something about dealing with pretty young women, maybe even some romance."

She gave him a little smile. "I suspect you know more about romance than you're letting on."

She's wrong about that, Tully thought. Just then Pap called to him and asked if he was done picking up snacks.

"That's my old father," Tully said. "Got some dementia, you know. I take him out of the home about once a month."

"I hope he doesn't think I'm one of your snacks," the lady said.

"Hard to tell what that crazy old codger might think."

"Well, it's been nice talking to you, but I've got to go." The lady started to walk away.

"Could I ask you one more question?" Tully called out.

The lady stopped and turned. "What's that?"

"What kind of men do the ladies in these Danielle Steel novels go for?"

She thought for a moment. "The men are always handsome, rich and powerful."

"Thanks," Tully said. One out of three ain't bad, he thought. He picked up two of the Danielle Steels and carried them up to the cashier, grabbing some candy bars and corn chips on the way. He watched through the front window as the lady drove off in her clean Sable.

He put the candy bars on the counter and held up the Steel novels for the girl at the cash register to see. She smiled and gave him a questioning look.

"They're for my father over there," he said, nodding toward Pap. "He loves these romance novels."

"What?" Pap said. "What's for me?"

"Nothing," Tully said. He shoved the books into the side pocket of his jacket.

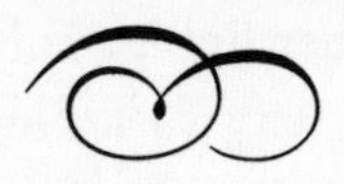

Chapter 18

Tully and Pap got into the Explorer and Tully turned out onto the highway.

"Where we headed now?" Pap asked. "Back to Blight City or the Littlefield ranch?"

"Something I want to check at the Littlefield ranch," Tully said. "Then I want to take a look at that skid trail where you found the ATV tracks."

When they reached a point where they could see the Littlefield ranch from the highway, Tully pulled into a turnout. He took his binoculars from the glove compartment and trained them on the ranch buildings. He moved the binoculars methodically from building to building.

"What you looking for?" Pap asked.

"A clean blue Mercury Sable," he said. "And I just found it. At least, the tail end of it, sticking out of a shed. Kincaid is closing the doors on it."

"That the Sable belonged to the lady you hit on back at the General Store?"

"I didn't hit on her. But, yeah, that's her Sable. Told me she was just passing through on her way to a new job in Boise. She's apparently connected to someone at the Littlefield ranch."

They drove back through Famine, on past the road to the Last Hope Mine and past the skid trail.

"I thought you wanted to take a look at the skid trail," Pap said.

"I do. But if the Littlefield crowd are somehow involved in this, I'm pretty sure they didn't drive their ATVs down the highway to get back to the ranch. Somebody might have seen them. There's got to be a place right up here where they pulled a truck in."

Then they saw it, a small picnic area alongside the river. The ice in the mud puddles of the entrance road had been broken and frozen again.

"Okay, this fits," Tully said. "They come out of the skid trail, drive a short distance down the road, and into the picnic area. Then they load the ATVs onto a truck, throw a tarp over them and drive back to the Littlefield ranch."

Pap said, "Or some farmhand could have forgot his lunch box and come in here with his truck to turn around."

"That, too," Tully said. "But there are ATV tracks all over. I prefer my version."

"It's good, all right," Pap said, "except we don't have the slightest bit of real evidence."

"At least the Littlefield ranch has ATVs."

"Every other person in this part of the county has an ATV."

"Stop demolishing my theories. Next time I'll leave you home. But if they left one ATV behind for the guy who killed Holt, the others would have had to wait here for him. Or he would have had to drive the ATV home. In that case, someone might have seen him. It would be pretty odd to see some fellow driving an ATV down the road at, say, four o'clock in the morning."

"Or they could have sent the truck back for him."

"That, too."

Tully turned around in the picnic area and drove back down the highway. Pap started making himself another cigarette.

They pulled off the highway onto a wide spot and then walked up the skid trail to where the ATVs had been parked. The skid trail didn't end at the mountain but continued on up the steep grade. Trees were now growing in parts of it, and the trail obviously hadn't been used since the days of horse logging. Tully walked carefully around the area where the ATVs had been parked. From the tracks, it was apparent the riders had turned them around, facing out down the trail.

"Looks as if they might have been prepared for a fast getaway," Tully said.

"That's what I thought," Pap said.

"So why would they have needed to make a fast getaway? It's the middle of night, they leave two dead guys in a car, one dead on a fence."

"Maybe they knew the guys in the car was pretty heavy dudes," Pap said. "Maybe they wasn't all that sure of themselves. Maybe they was a bunch of amateurs going up against some pros."

"Interesting point. And if these dead guys were pros from L.A., I suspect other pros in L.A. are going to send someone up to find out what happened to them."

"Whoever sent them up here, they already know what happened. Maybe they was the ambushers. Or they sent the ambushers."

"Stop! You're giving me a headache!"

He and Pap were walking out of the skid trail when Tully spotted something. He squatted down for a closer look. It was an unburned kitchen match but with what looked like teeth marks in it.

"Who chews kitchen matches anymore?" he said to Pap.

"Nobody I know," Pap said. "Don't even see kitchen matches around that much."

"Well, somebody up this trail not long ago was chewing on a kitchen match." Tully took out his handkerchief and carefully picked the match up by its head. Then he wrapped it loosely in the handkerchief and put it in his pocket.

"Don't mean whoever was chewing on the match was one of our killers, though," Pap said. "Could have been anybody."

"Would you shut up for once?" Tully said.

"Maybe after the county buys me lunch."

"Dave's House of Fry okay?"

"Perfect."

Tully's cell phone buzzed.

"My hunch was right," Buck said. "They did stop at the motel. Someone come in and reserved a couple rooms for them for two nights. An old guy in overalls, the manager said. Paid cash. Had on some stupid cap with earflaps. But that's all the description she could give. Three fellas in the Jeep stopped on their way through, maybe to use the bathroom. Weren't there more than fifteen minutes. The manager said she woke up and looked out the window. There were only three men, she said. The owners had left the cabins open, the keys on the tables inside. The men in the Jeep left the keys on the tables when they left and the cabins unlocked."

"Get out there and look around the cabins," Tully said. "Make sure they're secured when you leave."

"I'm on my way."

Tully slid the phone back in his jacket pocket and turned to Pap. "I've got to get myself some new people."

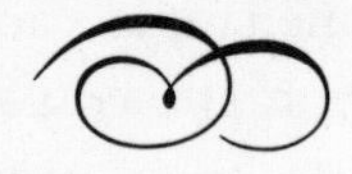

Chapter 19

Pap was having the liver-and-onions with bacon. Tully had ordered another chicken-fried steak. When something is that good, you keep on ordering it. He had forgotten how big the steak was. It overlapped the sides of the plate.

Dave came over to their table and sat down. Deedee brought refills for Pap and Tully and poured a cup for Dave.

"You got the crime solved yet?" Dave said.

"Don't I wish," Tully said.

"Bo lets it stretch out anymore, I'm gonna get sick of it," Pap said. "Back in the old days we'd have had someone locked up by now."

"And probably tried and hanged," Tully said, cutting into his steak. "But I'd kind of like to get the guys who actually did it."

"Well, if you're gonna be picky," Pap said, forking a chunk of liver into his mouth.

"You got any suspects, Bo?" Dave asked.

"Not really. But there is something funny going on out at the Littlefield ranch. Most of Vern's crew has been let go and all he's got left are two fellows who can't tell one end of a cow from the other."

"Vern told me that he was going broke with cattle," Dave said. "Says the thing nowadays is grapes. He's turning the whole ranch into vineyards."

"I don't think the guys he's got left have ever stomped a grape, either," Tully said. "I met his new wife, too. Cindy. Got a ferret she lets run around inside her blouse."

"Ain't that something," Dave said. "First time I saw her blouse move like that I thought he must have picked Cindy up at a circus. Then this ferret sticks his head out her sleeve. He was smiling, too."

Tully laughed and the old man almost choked on his liver-and-onions.

"I'll bet he was smiling," Tully said. "She looks about sixteen but she admits to thirty-four."

At that moment Deedee blurted out a twelve-letter obscenity, leaped back from a table of locals and dumped a tray of dishes on the floor. Then she started to cry, rubbing her rear end. The obvious culprit was grinning at her, but his companions seemed more embarrassed than amused. A couple of them glanced over at Dave.

"You want me to handle this?" Tully said.

"Would you?" Dave said. "I'm kind of tired today."

Tully got up and walked over to the man. He kept his jacket buttoned to hide the badge. "You pinch her?" he asked.

The man leaped up and stuck his face up against Tully's.

"You think this is any of your business, pal, let's see you do something about it."

"I don't mean to interfere, mister," Pap called out. "But you better get out of his face!"

The warning came too late. Tully could already feel that strange numbing sensation creeping up his right arm.

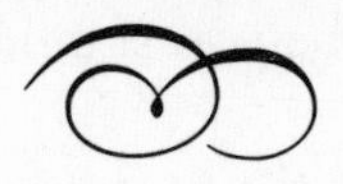

Chapter 20

As they passed the sign that said "Blight City, Pop. 16,350," Pap read it aloud, as if seeing it for the first time. "Sixteen thousand three hundred and fifty."

It seemed to Tully that the old man read the sign aloud every time they passed it. "Strange," he said. "The town hasn't grown a bit since we left."

"It hasn't grown in seventy-five years," Pap said.

"Then why do you read it every time we pass?"

"Just to annoy you," Pap said.

Pap started making himself a cigarette. He paused for a moment and offered the opinion that Tully should have hauled in the guy for pinching Deedee. "That's assault," he said. He had referred to the man by the same obscenity Deedee had used, although he usually avoided such extremes.

"Naw," Tully said. "I doubt Dave will ever let him back in his establishment. And that's the only decent place to eat anywhere near Famine."

"I'm not sure that's punishment. Maybe you should have let Dave handle it, then."

"You ever see Dave handle a situation like that?"

"Can't say I have. Why?"

"Dave doesn't have an 'Off' button, that's why. He starts, he can't stop. That's why he almost always lets somebody else handle a situation."

"Where we headed now?" Pap said.

"Back to the Pine Creek Motel. You want to go home first?"

"I'll hang out a while. Never can tell when you might need my help."

They stopped at the Pine Creek Motel. Earlier in the year there had actually been a creek behind the Pine Creek Motel, but it had dried up into a series of puddles over the summer. Janet Simmons, the owner, had set out several little picnic tables with benches for her guests. Half the rooms had sliding doors that opened out to the tables. Tully had dated Janet for a while, as he had almost all the women in Blight. Most of the relationships had ended the same way—not well. The breakup with Janet had been one of the more public and spectacular. It was still recalled with considerable amusement by the other diners at Crabbs Restaurant that evening. Tully wished he'd had time to read Danielle Steel before stopping by the Pine Creek.

The old pickup trucks were still parked outside the motel, but there was no sign of the ranch hands. He hoped they hadn't simply left the trucks and ridden a bus out of town.

"No," Janet told him. "They're still here. I put them

in four rooms, which are costing the county a hundred and fifty dollars a day."

Tully shuddered, thinking about explaining the bills to the county commissioners. "Hope they haven't caused you any trouble," he said.

Janet laughed, rather bitterly, Tully thought. "No, I've had no trouble from *them*. They've been nice and polite."

"So, you got any idea where they might be right now?"

"They're wandering around town, I expect. They eat over at Granny's three times a day, poor devils, but then they just wander around. Don't know what there is about Blight City that could interest them so much. Oh, wait, here they come now."

Tully glanced in the direction Janet had nodded. The little band of cowboys had just come into sight around a corner. They wore jeans, denim jackets, and battered hats with the edges of the brims rolled up. Their faces brightened when they saw him. They smiled and waved at Pap, who had remained in the Explorer. The old man raised his hand in greeting.

Tully said, "I hope the lady proprietor here hasn't been too mean to you."

"No, she's very nice," Pete Barton said. "But I got to tell you, Sheriff, this is one boring town. We looked it over end to end three times already, and it's even more boring than I always thought it was."

"It livens up on Saturday nights," Tully said.

"But not so much anyone would notice," Janet said. She walked back into the motel office.

"You can take off today, if you want. But let me know where I can find you. You can write it down, Pete, and leave it with Ms. Simmons in there. She's a friend of mine."

"I don't think so," Pete said.

"Why not?"

"I mean, I don't think she is a friend of yours."

"Hmmm. I do have a couple of questions for you, Pete. Did Vern Littlefield give you any reason why he was letting you go?"

"Nope, never said a word about it. He did mention a couple of times he was getting out of the cattle business. But he still had several hundred head. The two guys he's got left know nothing about cattle. Mostly they just rode around on ATVs. They didn't stay with us. I think they moved into the other big house at the main ranch, where Littlefield's parents lived before they died."

"I wondered about that, too," Tully said.

"One of the men, Bob Mitchell, might have known the new wife," Pete said.

"Why do you say that?"

"When Vern's gone, they hang out together. Maybe it's nothing. It just seemed strange. We'd see them in a pickup truck, headed to town. Like that. I don't think they was having an affair or anything. Every time I seen her go by in a truck with Mitchell, she looked mighty unhappy."

"Which town?"

"Famine. Sometimes Blight City."

"How long would they be gone?"

"I don't know. We didn't pay that much attention.

Once, though, they didn't come back until it was nearly dark."

"You all know Vern Littlefield pretty well," Tully said. "I guess he really loves his elk hunting."

"I don't know about that," Pete said. "I think he likes to go up to the camp just to hang out all by himself for a few days. My guess is, he mostly pretends to hunt anymore."

"You got any idea what gun he might take?"

"Vern wasn't the kind of guy who would hang around and shoot the bull with us about hunting or anything else, but one time we set up a little range for sighting in our own rifles, and he came out and sighted in one of his. It was a scoped Remington two-seventy."

"How about Mitchell's partner, that Harry Kincaid? You know anything about him?"

"Nope. He and Bob Mitchell showed up here about four years ago. Never do any work. Can't tell one end of a cow from the other. Kincaid is one cold dude. Hardly ever says a word, just gives you that cold stare, when you speak to him. He'd be out on the ranch sometimes at night, hunting coyotes. He knew how to call them in with one of them little game calls. He must have shot dozens. Sometimes he wouldn't even bother to haul them in to Whitey's Furs, just let 'em lay. Whitey would give us twenty-five to forty dollars, depending on the size and condition of the coyote we shot. He would knock off five dollars if the exit wound was too big, so we started using exploding tips. Those bullets don't exit at all. For what they call a Pale Montana, that's kind of a light cream-colored coyote, Whitey would give us seventy-five dollars, if it didn't have a big exit wound. I found a Pale Montana shot weeks before and left to rot by Kincaid. Can you imagine that, just leaving seventy-five dollars out there to waste? Made me sick."

"You ever notice what kind of gun Kincaid was using on the coyotes?"

"Nope, I never did. I got a Ruger Ranch Rifle myself. It's a great varmint gun."

"Accurate?"

"Shoot a flea off a dog's back at a hundred yards."

"The two-twenty-three is what some SWAT teams use," Tully said. "Our guys are trained to do the 'double tap,' two shots in the middle of the body mass. I prefer the pelvis myself. Bullets hit that hard bone down there and go round and round. Put a man down a lot faster than two shots in the chest, at least in my opinion."

"Sounds awful."

"It is awful. But when you've got somebody trying to kill you, you don't think about that."

"Two shots! Well, I guess if coyotes came armed, I'd want to use two shots myself."

The other three cowboys were sprawled out on the benches of one of Janet Simmons's picnic tables. Their deaths from boredom seemed imminent.

"I appreciate the information, Pete," Tully said. "I guess you all can take off for Texas right now if you want. Leave a note with Ms. Simmons, so I'll know how to reach you if I need to. One more question. Did you notice where Mitchell and Kincaid rode the ATVs?"

"Mostly up in the Hoodoo Mountains behind the ranch. Old dirt logging roads go every which way back there. You probably could drive them all the way to Blight City, if you knew what roads to take."

"You ever been on those roads?"

"Sure. A few years ago, Vern and me would go up there sometimes looking for timber to cut. He would pick out the trees and I'd mark them, and later some of us would go up and cut them. The trees didn't amount to much. Hardly seemed worth the trouble to cut and haul them."

"What would he do with the logs?"

"Don't rightly know. Guess he'd sell them. Not much else he could do with them. He has a self-loader on a truck, and he'd haul the logs himself."

Tully held out his hand and Pete shook it. "I'm glad you stayed in town," Tully said. "For a while there I thought you all might head on down the road."

Pete and the others laughed. "We thought about it, all right. And then your officer, Undersheriff Eliot, drove over and told us to stop thinking about it. So we stopped thinking about it."

"Good idea," Tully said.

Chapter 21

Tully dropped Pap off at his home and then drove over to his own place. His log house sat in the middle of a meadow surrounded by eighty timbered acres. He and his wife, Ginger, had built the house themselves, log by log. They had been married for nearly ten years. Then Ginger suddenly got sick and died. Something had burst in her brain. She was thirty-two. She was the only person who had ever made Tully feel as if he belonged to someone. She would often walk behind him when he hunted pheasants and quail. She didn't like hunting and never carried a gun. She just wanted to share in that part of his life, his doing something he loved. In the ten years since, there had never been a time when he hadn't felt alone. Only since Gail had stormed out on him had he started feeling good about being alone. It was all right to feel alone.

A brick chimney rose straight up through the open rafters of the house between the kitchen and the living room. A wood range was piped into the chimney on one side and a wood heater on the other. Two bedrooms and two baths were off one side of the living room. The kitchen window overlooked a small stream that meandered down through a grove of birch. Tully still heated and cooked with wood, which he cut with a chain saw. He cut cottonwood and quaking aspen for the range, because it burned hot and fast, and birch for the heater, because it burned longer and cooler and because his property contained a lot of birch. Originally, he and Ginger had intended the house to be self-sufficient, so they could survive as artists, he as a painter and she as a potter. Later, they added electric baseboard heaters. "Just in case," Ginger had said. "Just in case" had been one of her favorite phrases. She liked to have a backup. Tully sometimes wondered if she had a backup for him, and exactly what that might be. Ginger was a much more social person than he. She had loved parties and dancing and hayrides through the snow with friends at Christmas, all of which Tully could easily have done without. Ginger also had trouble with common sayings, which she would change only slightly, thereby adding to the confusion. Water always passed over Ginger's bridges, not under. "Well, that's water over the bridge," she'd say. Perhaps that was more appropriate for life with Tully. His bridge always seemed to be half underwater, anyway.

"You're just an old stink in the mud," she had said once, in response to his refusal to attend some social function.

"Stick," he had said. "The expression is 'stick in the mud.'"

"Stick!" she said. "That doesn't make any sense."

"Neither does stink."

"Yes, it does! In your case, anyway!"

Tully stuffed some paper, cedar kindling and a few small pieces of birch into the heater and lit the paper. The fire was soon crackling away. He plopped into his rocker in front of it and watched the flames leap and dance behind the tiny glass window in the door. Someday he would sell the place. But not quite yet. He wasn't ready yet.

The phone rang. He walked over and picked it up from his desk in the corner of the living room. "Tully here."

"Hi, Sheriff. This is Susan Parker. I got your home number from Daisy Quinn. She said she didn't think you'd mind."

"The pleasure is all mine."

"I thought you might be interested in the result of the autopsies. Holt, the guy over the fence, probably died about four in the morning, but it's difficult to get any closer with body temperature, because it was so cold that night. As you know, we can pin the time of death of the two victims in the car to exactly three thirty-eight, because one bullet hit the driver's watch. Assuming Holt got out of the car, he would have died after that."

"How about the bullets?"

"The two men in the car were killed with nine-millimeter full-metal-jacket bullets, military rounds. Passing through the car door pretty well wiped out any useful striations. The guns had to be automatics, probably with thirty-round magazines, strictly illegal, if that makes a difference. Might have been Uzis. Cause of death was multiple gunshot wounds, as you would expect. Holt, the guy at the fence, was killed with two-twenty-three-caliber rounds with exploding tips. As you probably know, they're like hollow points but with a plastic plug in the hole. The base of the bullets remained intact, though, and we've got good striations there. All you have to do is find the rifle that fired the rounds and we can get a match. That fits with the casing Dave found by the gatepost, a two-twenty-three. Because the two bullet holes are so close together, I suspect they came from a semiautomatic rifle. Neither slug exited. You find any more evidence?"

"A matchstick I may want you to send to the Idaho Crime Lab to see if they can pick up any DNA off of it. Also, I'd like the lab to see if they can give us a match between that pool of blood in the woods and the patch of blood on the skid trail."

"Anything else?"

"Not much. I'm pretty sure drugs are involved with this whole scene, but I haven't figured out how. Anyway, would you consider having dinner with me tonight? We could kick this whole thing around for a while."

"Sure. I'm not going to get wrapped up with work over here until about seven, if that's okay."

"Where can I pick you up?"

"I don't have an apartment yet. Right now I'm staying at the Goddard Bed and Breakfast. I assume you know where that is."

Bad news. Tully had once dated Carol Smiley, back before she had married that clown, Rich Goddard. "You bet. How does eight sound?"

"Super. That will give me time to shower."

She at least left Tully with a pleasant image, one that could go a long way toward erasing his images of her carving up dead bodies. But not quite.

He hung up his jacket and eased into his rocking chair with one of the Danielle Steels. He read three chapters and then started thumbing through the book, looking for useful advice. Then he saw it: "He looked at her warmly." Nothing too smarmy, just a look. This has to be it, he thought. Just a look, a way of looking. He couldn't remember ever looking at a woman warmly. Hungrily, perhaps, but not warmly. He walked into the bathroom and tried out his warm look in the mirror. It was harder than he had expected. He practiced it a few times, until he had it down. Someday he'd read more of the Danielle Steel, but so far he had found it almost painfully boring.

He phoned the office. Daisy said there were no new developments, except the usual reports of prowlers and chainsaw thefts. He told her to get hold of Buck and have him return to Blight City for the night. Then he showered and shaved and put on fresh clothes—gray slacks, a black shirt and his black leather jacket. He slipped into his black loafers, which felt surprisingly light and comfortable after his boots. Tying a length of paper towels around his neck, he trimmed a few unruly hairs from his mustache and eyebrows. His hair was a bit long. He checked his watch. Four o'clock. He still had time to stop by Clyde's Barber Shop for a trim. He held his hands up to the bathroom light. The knuckles of his right hand were bruised and cracked. Well, nothing he could do about that.

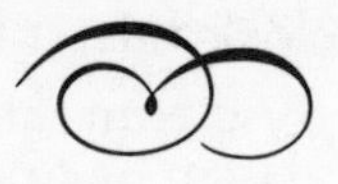

Chapter 22

Clyde Swartze and Everett Barnes were sweeping up the barber shop when Tully walked in.

"Got time for a quick trim?" he asked.

"Always got time for the sheriff," Clyde said. He indicated his chair. "Have a seat, Bo. How come you're all dolled up? Off on one of your infamous dates?"

"None of your business, Clyde. Just give me a nice neat trim and watch out for the ears."

Everett sat down in his own chair and began to read the paper. He was about twenty-five and skinny and already going bald.

Clyde tied a paper slip and a big blue barber's cape around Tully's neck. "How's your murder investigation going up in Famine, Bo?"

"It's going, Clyde. That's about all I know."

"You figure it's got something to do with drugs?"

"Maybe, but we've never had much of a drug problem in Blight."

"A lot of money in the drug industry," Clyde said.

"Yeah," Everett said, "I seen in the paper where the cops up in Spokane busted some wealthy housewives for growing pot in their houses with grow lights. I guess the cops figured out the women were using about five times as much electricity as they should have been. You'd think some of the folks around here would show that kind of initiative."

"I hate to crush your hopes, Ev," Tully said, "but Blight County is too cold for much of a drug industry."

"It's always something," Clyde said.

A story about food stamps in the paper caught Everett's attention. "Boy, if there's one thing I hate to see, it's people using food stamps."

"Why is that, Ev?" Tully asked.

"If they'd get out and get a job, they wouldn't need food stamps. They're just lazy. I hate like the devil to be supporting them."

"I know what you mean," Tully said. "I ever tell you my theory about poverty, Ev?"

"I don't think so, Bo."

"I've heard it," Clyde said. "And I bet I'm going to hear it again."

"Yes, you are, Clyde. It goes like this. First thing we need to do is to withdraw all support from poor people. If they can't earn their own way, they starve."

"I'm for that," Everett said.

"Of course," Tully went on, "we wouldn't want women and children and babies and old people starving to death out in public, all bony and their eyes bulging out and like that. I mean that would be disgusting. It would be uncivilized, don't you think, Ev?"

Ev nodded mutely, no longer looking at his paper but staring out the shop's front window, as if imagining people starving to death on Blight City's Main Street.

"No, sir," Tully went on, "what we would need is some kind of warehouse, out in the country maybe, where we could put the poor people who were starving to death, get them out of sight, for heaven's sake, don't you think, Ev?"

Ev said, "I don't think I'd go that far."

Tully glanced in the mirror. "Maybe a little more off the top, Clyde." He looked over at the young barber, who was still staring out the front window.

"Hold still, Bo," Clyde said.

"Sorry," Tully said. "I just get carried away every time I hear about food stamps. You don't like the warehouse idea? That's awfully hard, Ev, awfully hard. You'd just let the folks starve to death out there in the street?"

"No, I mean I don't like the idea of letting them starve."

"I never said curing poverty would be easy. And I wouldn't look forward to hauling starving poor folks off to the warehouse. But I would do it. It would just be too disgusting having them die out here in public. By the way, Ev, you're not one of them bleeding-heart liberals, are you?"

Everett shook his head no.

"Good."

"You want any cream or anything on your hair, Bo?" Clyde asked.

"Maybe just a tiny bit of tonic, Clyde. Not too much, though, because I've got a business engagement tonight."

"Anyone I know?" Clyde said.

"I hope not," Tully said.

Clyde undid the cape and paper strip from around Tully's neck. "There you go, Bo, good as new. That'll be eight bucks."

"Eight bucks! Boy, speaking of folks getting robbed!"

He gave the barber a ten, slipped on his jacket and started out the door. He stopped suddenly and turned back toward the young barber. "You sure you're not one of them liberals, Ev?"

Everett was still staring out into the street. He shook his head no. "But I'm not totally against food stamps," he said.

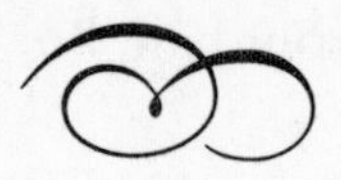

Chapter 23

The restaurant was packed. Fortunately, the owner, Charlie Crabb, had reserved Tully's usual table for him off in a quiet corner. A small lamp shaped like a lantern threw a red light over the tablecloth. Crabbs was the only restaurant in town with actual tablecloths. Both Charlie and Tully thought it gave the place a touch of class. Tully didn't much care for the waitpersons, who seemed to project an attitude that the diners had been granted a considerable privilege to spend their money at Crabbs.

"I thought there would be crab on the menu at Crabbs," Susan said, obviously disappointed.

"Afraid not," Tully said. "As you can see from the menu, this is basically red-meat country. I do recommend the prime rib, though."

"Thanks," she said, "but I've had enough red meat for one day. Maybe I'll go with the catfish."

"Good choice," Tully said. Susan's red-meat image

had taken the edge off his appetite. "I think I'll have that, too."

"So what do you think that business at the Last Hope Mine Road was all about?" she asked.

"I don't have much of an idea yet," he said. "The clothes, the money, the fact that all the dead guys were from L.A., make me think drugs had to be involved. But we've never had much of a drug problem in Blight County. For one thing, most folks here are so poor they can't afford drugs. Maybe that's the reason they have such a dim view of them. A known drug dealer here would not be viewed highly. Blight is still pretty much back in the fifties, particularly in regard to dope fiends."

"Dope fiends! It's been a long time since I've heard that term."

"It's one of my favorites."

"So you're also an artist?"

"Yes. Actually, I like to think of myself as an artist working as a sheriff." He took a sip of his water. One thing about Blight City, it still had good water.

"That seems reasonable," Susan said. "So what kind of artist are you?"

"Painter," Tully said. "Oils and watercolors." He didn't like to discuss his art, particularly on a first date.

"The folks around Blight must be pretty impressed at having a sheriff who paints."

"I wouldn't say that. I get a chance, I head up along the West Branch with my watercolors. Sometimes when I can get away, I'll camp out up there for a week and do nothing but fish and paint."

"Sounds nice."

A waitress came to take their drink orders. Tully ordered a bottle of white merlot. “You want anything?” he asked Susan.

She laughed. “I think I’ll just drink some of your merlot.”

“Two glasses then,” he told the waitress.

“Vern Littlefield,” he went on, “is apparently switching from cows to grapes. We may soon have our own Blight County Winery.”

“Sounds like a step in the right direction,” Susan said.

A waiter came and permitted them to order dinner. Susan ordered the catfish with garlic mashed potatoes. Tully said, “Same for me.” They both took the salad bar. When they returned from the salad bar, Susan dipped a carrot stick in a pool of ranch dressing and munched it daintily, her brow furrowing up with a question. “So what’s the plan?”

“Plan?” Tully said.

“Your plan. Everybody should have a plan. Like, do you plan to be a sheriff forever or are you going to be an artist?”

Tully laughed. “It may surprise you to learn that most of the folks in Blight County don’t have a plan. It never occurs to them not to stay right here doing what they do or don’t do forever and never to change if they can help it.”

“Does that include you?”

“I don’t know. I like sheriffing and I like painting. I suppose if I became famous, I mean *when* I become famous, I might move somewhere else, but it’s very, very hard to become famous in Blight County. Folks here are pretty much denied their fifteen minutes of fame."

"Well, do you ever sell your paintings or do you just keep them piled up in a back room? Or on the walls of the courthouse?"

Tully munched a piece of his catfish. "One thing about Charlie Crabb, he knows how to cook catfish. How's yours?"

"Lovely. But I asked if you ever sell your paintings?"

"Yes, I do. Every year I sell a few more. There's a gallery in L.A. that sells two or three a year. One of these days, the gallery is going to give me a one-man show. Every year I go down to L.A. for a week or so and hobnob around the art circles. The owner of the gallery introduces me to the L.A. arty folk, who seem to find it amusing that the sheriff of a little Idaho county is also a painter. Maybe one day I'll give up sheriffing and paint full time, if I can find a rich woman to support me. By the way, Susan, are you rich?"

"Nope. Sorry. My folks are pretty well off, though. They sent me to Stanford, where I majored in chemistry. Then I went to medical school, where I specialized in forensic medicine. And here I am."

"How about your plan?

"If I can find a rich man to support me, maybe I'll stay home and fuss about in my garden. Right now, I don't have either a home or a garden, or for that matter a rich man to support me."

"Sounds like a pretty sad situation to me," Tully said.

"You don't happen to be rich, do you?" Susan said.

"Afraid not. But I do have hopes of someday discovering a nice little gold mine."

Susan laughed. "Be sure to look me up as soon as you find it."

Tully thought this was the perfect moment to try out his warm look. He leaned forward and gave it his best shot.

Susan looked startled. "Are you all right, Bo? Are you sick?"

Tully instantly shut off his warm look. "I'm fine, I'm fine. Just caught something in my throat."

"You looked terrible there for a second. I thought you were going to erp all over the table."

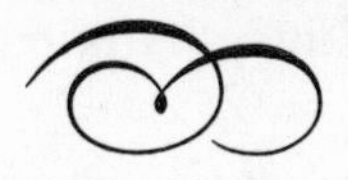

Chapter 24

Tully got into the office at eight sharp. He was carrying a paper sack.

For once there was some hot coffee and a couple of fresh doughnuts. He answered a few questions and issued some orders to his deputies before they headed out on assignments. He glanced over at the corner of the briefing room, but Lurch was out. Herb Eliot came over and stood in the sheriff's office doorway while Tully checked the window for flies. A couple of mediums were up near the top of the glass. Tully popped one of them, caught it with the swatter in mid-fall and rolled it out on the sill. He stood his finger on the sill. Two sharp raps with the handle of the swatter brought Wallace scurrying out. He stopped in front of the finger. Tully examined him. He looked a little peaked.

"Daisy, you been feeding my spider?"

"Yes," she yelled back. "I fed him, didn't I, Herb?"

"Is that right, Herb? You wouldn't lie to me now,

just to protect a pretty girl from a serious spanking, would you?"

"Hmmm. Would I get to watch the spanking, Sheriff?"

"That could be arranged."

"Tell the truth, Herb!" Daisy said.

"Darn it all to heck, Sheriff, she did feed your spider."

"You could spank me anyway," Daisy said.

Tully laughed and raised his finger. Wallace raced in, grabbed the fly and hauled it back into his den behind the filing cabinet.

"So how was Batim country?" Eliot asked.

"Pretty bad, actually. A bit too much killing, even for Pap."

"That bad, hunh? Well, we've certainly been mobbed by the press about the murders."

"Mobbed! Really?"

"Three newspaper reporters, plus Barney from the *Blight Bugle*. A Spokane television station sent down a photographer and a reporter, a girl. I gave her an interview. Hope that was okay."

"He did really good, Bo," Daisy said.

"You mention to the reporters how long before you had the murders solved?" Tully asked.

"I probably did," Eliot said. "Actually, I was so nervous I can't remember what I told them. Maybe I said I had already solved them."

"What did you look like on TV?"

"We don't get that channel down here, but I must have looked pretty good. How could I not? So, did the

Scraggs have anything to do with that mess up in Famine?"

"Don't know. It's possible. Which reminds me, first, call the LAPD and see if they've got anything on our three vics. When you get around to it, find somebody who can tell you what the average snowfall has been for, say, the last five years."

"Will do. You worried about that Cliff kid?"

"Who?"

"The Cliff kid. Ran off to the mountains again. Probably already got quite a bit of snow up where he's hiding out."

"Yeah, well, I can find him anytime I want. Right now I've got other stuff to worry about. Where did they put that car the wrecker hauled in from the Last Hope Mine Road?"

"The city garage. Nobody knew what to do with it, so I said put it there."

"Good enough. Lurch go over it anymore?"

"Yeah, he's over there right now. I think he's running some experiment you wanted him to do."

Tully set the paper sack on his desk. "Good. I'm heading back up to Famine. When Lurch gets in, have him check the stuff in the sack for prints. There's also some samples there that need to go to the crime lab for DNA analysis. I've got them all marked, but Lurch will know which is which."

"You got it."

"Daisy, call Pap and tell him we're going to head back up to Famine. I'll pick him up in about an hour. Exactly one hour."

"Okay, but I don't think he likes me very much."

"Don't worry about that. His bite is a good deal worse than his bark. Just don't let him get close enough to bite."

"You want him armed?"

"He's always armed, sweetheart. It was foolish of me to think differently."

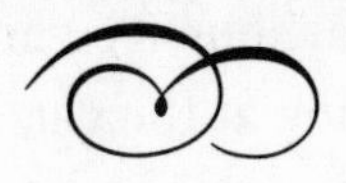

Chapter 25

Tully walked over to the medical examiner's office. Susan was sitting at a large wooden table looking over some photographs. He avoided looking at the photographs, just in case he decided to have a late breakfast. He walked up behind her and touched her on the shoulder. She jumped.

"Sorry," he said. "I didn't mean to startle you."

"These murders have got me jumpy, I guess. What brings you over here?" she asked.

Tully was still a little embarrassed from his failed attempt at a warm look. "So what have we got now?"

"I'm not sure how interesting it is. About the same as I told you on the phone. Holt was killed by two two-twenty-three-caliber bullets, both from the back. The bullets had exploding tips, but the base on each was in good shape, good enough to be matched to a rifle. The shooter was pretty good. He knew what he was doing."

"How about time of death for Holt?"

"Really hard to be accurate about that, but we can pin it to about a half hour after the shooting at the car."

"Any of the slugs in the bodies at the car in good enough shape that we can get a positive identification of the guns that fired them?"

"No, the car door messed them up too much."

"That's okay, we have the shell casings. Now all we have to do is find the guns in possession of whoever did the shooting."

"Got any idea who that might be?"

"Not a smidgen. In any case, Pap and I and Buck are headed back up to Famine today. There's something very strange going on up there. You want to come?"

"I'd love to, but I'm totally beat. Besides, I've got to find an apartment or some other place to live."

Tully wondered to himself if she was hinting that she move in with him.

"No," she said. "I wasn't hinting that."

He had to remember to stop tugging on his mustache while he had deep thoughts in front of perceptive women.

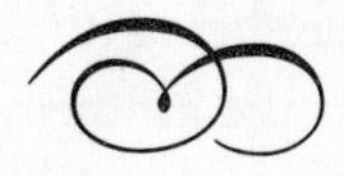

Chapter 26

Pap was sitting in the rocker on his front porch when Tully pulled up. He had his pack and his cooler alongside him. The old man must have had enough of the cold, because he was wearing his old red mackinaw, black wool pants and a black wool watch cap. Tully was pretty sure he also had his red long johns on.

After once again going through the business with the seat belt, and Tully fastening it for him, Pap got himself settled into the Explorer and started making himself a cigarette. Tully no longer bothered to complain.

"You got it all figured out?" Pap said.

"Making some headway. One way or another, Vern Littlefield is involved. But maybe he's just another victim."

"You don't think he's the fourth man?"

"He could be. Here we have these three guys from L.A. letting themselves be steered up the Last Hope Mine Road in the middle of the night. Why? It must be that they were going to be shown something. Or at least thought they were. It's pretty clear they were being lured out to that road on some pretext, and that the ambushers were waiting for them."

Pap lit his cigarette with the Explorer's lighter and blew a cloud of smoke against the windshield. "You said all that's up that road is a dinky little dam and a mine that's been blown shut. What could they want to look at, the L.A. guys?"

"Beats me. I guess they could be told just about anything. The three victims look to me like the sort of folks who get the bends if they stray outside L.A.'s smog belt. I don't think they thought they were out there to view the stars from a mountaintop." Tully wondered if Susan might like to view the stars from a mountaintop.

"You check them out with the LAPD?"

"Herb did. They've all got records up to their clavicles. Of late, they've been involved with drugs. Before that, just about anything illegal. The L.A. detective Herb talked to didn't seem too upset when he heard about their sudden demise."

"I suppose not," Pap said. "By the way, not to change the subject, but how did your date with Susan go?"

"How did you hear about that?"

"I keep my ear to the ground."

"When there's no keyhole to keep your eye to. Well, you know how it is. Sure, women find me extremely attractive, but Susan and I are happy enough just to be good friends."

"So how did you mess up this time?"

"Beats the heck out of me."

Chapter 27

Tully dropped Pap off in Famine to ask some questions around town. Then he headed out to the Littlefield ranch. Cindy Littlefield answered the door and invited him in. As far as he could tell, the ferret wasn't at the moment roaming around under her blouse.

"I have a few questions for Vern," Tully said. "He make it back?"

"No, he hasn't. I've been getting a little worried about him."

Tully glanced around the living room, taking in the gigantic fireplace, big-screen TV, hardwood floors, leather couch and easy chairs, expensive lamps, nice art on the walls, one watercolor in particular.

"You have good taste in art," he said.

"Vern does, anyway. I'm not into home decorating, at least not yet."

Home decorating! Just as he had suspected, Cindy

Littlefield could cut a guy down to size, even if she didn't intend to.

"You expect Vern back soon?"

"Actually, I expected him back the evening you were here. You know Dave Perkins? He's a friend of Vern's, so I called him and asked if he would go up to the hunting camp and check on Vern. He stopped by later and said Vern's pickup truck was there, but Vern wasn't."

"If he said he was going elk hunting, maybe he was talking about a spike camp farther up in the mountains."

"I don't know about any spike camp. What is that?"

"Usually it's just a tent and some gear, a place to eat and sleep while you're hunting elk. Saves you the trouble of getting yourself back into the high mountains every morning."

"I don't know. I've never been up to the hunting camp. If his pickup is there, he must be."

"I'm sure he's all right," Tully said, although he wasn't. "He's been roaming these mountains since he was a little kid. Been out with him myself a few times, when I was a youngster. Anyway, I had only a couple of questions for Vern. Maybe you can answer them."

"I doubt it, but I'll try."

"How often did Vern go up to his dam?"

"Maybe every couple of weeks."

"And how long has that been?"

"About six months."

"Where did you meet Vern?"

"Los Angeles. I worked at a small private airport

near the city, and Vern would fly in from time to time. He asked me out to dinner one day, and pretty soon he started flying in a lot more."

"Before he met you, what was he doing down there, business things?"

"He never said. And I never asked."

"When did he start to sell off his cattle?"

"Oh, those stupid cows! They are about to drive us bankrupt. He's been getting rid of them the last few months. The old crew were all good cowboys. I don't know why he decided to let them go, when we still have hundreds of cattle left."

"So the fellows I met here the other day, they're the grape people?"

"Mitchell is someone he hired to help manage the ranch. Maybe he's supposed to set up the wine operation, if that's what comes next. Vern never tells me much about his plans."

"I see there are two planes out there? Is one of them Mitchell's?"

"That's right. He and Kincaid flew in one day and pretty much stayed. They were traveling back and forth to the ranch long before I got here."

"Kind of odd Vern would go off elk hunting, with all these changes going on."

"I suppose. But if Vern sets his mind to do something, he does it. He must have had his mind set on elk hunting."

"So he just got up one morning and took off on his hunt?"

"Well, he was out all hours of the night with his friends and when he got home I guess he just packed up and left. He was gone by the time I got up."

"If you don't get your elk around here, you're practically nobody," Tully said.

Cindy laughed. "I guess. Can I get you something to drink, Sheriff?"

"Nope, I've got to go. I left my father loose in town. But have Vern give me a call when he shows up."

He gave her the number of his cell phone, even though he no longer expected Vern to show up.

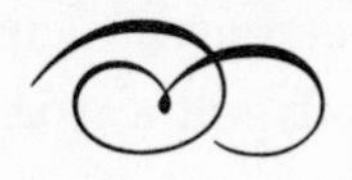

Chapter 28

Buck's Explorer was parked alongside Ed's Gas-N-Grub. Tully could see Buck and Pap inside, sprawled in chairs, drinking coffee and talking to Ed.

"I hope you fellas aren't overdoing it," he said, coming through the door and looking around. Ed's pretty cashier was apparently taking the day off.

"Buck and I canvassed the whole town," Pap said. "Knocked on practically every door. Nobody knows nothing. You find out anything from Littlefield?"

"Nope. He's still out on his elk hunt."

"Elk hunt?" Ed said. "You'd think he had enough to do, starting a vineyard and all."

"His wife asked Dave Perkins to go up and look for him at his hunting camp," Tully told them. "Dave apparently found Vern's pickup truck up there, but no Vern."

Someone drove over the hose out front and a bell chimed in the station. Ed went out to wait on the customer.

"Ed's still stuck back in the last century," Pap observed. "He pumps the gas, checks the oil, and washes the windshield, side and rear windows. Even wipes off the headlights."

"You mean gas station people used to do all that stuff?" Buck said.

"You bet," Pap said. "Only in Famine do you still get waited on at a gas station like you was some kind of royalty."

"What'd they charge for that kind of service?" Buck asked.

"Nothing. But of course gas did cost fifteen cents a gallon."

"No way!" Buck looked at Tully for confirmation.

"Don't look at me, Buck. Listen, while Ed's out front, this is just between the three of us, okay?"

Buck and Pap nodded.

"I think maybe Vern Littlefield was the person standing back in the woods and got hit. It's pretty odd that Vern suddenly went elk hunting the night of the shooting and hasn't shown up since."

"I don't get you, Bo," Buck said. "Why would he go elk hunting if he got shot?"

Pap stared silently at Buck.

"What I'm getting at, Buck, is that Vern really didn't go hunting. That's just an excuse whoever's involved in this thought up to explain his disappearance."

"It's a good one, too," Pap said. "Elk hunters around here go missing right often, particularly if they have a young, pretty wife. You think she's involved, Bo?"

"Don't know. There are those two big-city chaps staying at the ranch. They don't seem to be of much use to anyone. Plus there's that lady who pulled in there the other day. Looked like they were hiding her car in one of the sheds. I didn't see her today, so she may have gone on to Boise."

"Well, I guess you've been doing some snooping," Pap said.

"Pap, you know anybody over at Central Electric management?"

"No, nobody who knows anything. Why?"

"I need some information, but I guess I can call Paul Cooper over there. The problem is, if I call Paul, I'll have to talk fishing."

"You know how to talk fishing."

"Not catch-and-release fishing."

"Catch-and-release? What's that?"

"I didn't think you'd know. Anyway, here comes Ed."

Ed shook his head as he came through the door. "Only place left in the world," he said, "where a person can still order three dollars' worth of gas."

"And get his windows washed and his oil checked to boot," Pap said. "By the way, Ed, how come you got only two pumps, regular and extra, but no premium?"

"Saves me money. If I had premium, nobody in Famine would buy it anyway. So I don't have to have a tank for it, and tanks are expensive. I do have a diesel pump. Keep it out back, where the logging trucks can get to it."

"Sounds reasonable," Pap said.

"We had better get going," Tully said. "Buck, you drive Pap."

"I'd love to drive the old devil. Where you going, Bo?"

"Thought I'd stop in and have a chat with Batim Scragg."

"Maybe I should go with you," Buck said. "I wouldn't mind bashing a few Scragg heads."

"Bo can bash any heads that need bashing," Pap said.

"Yeah, but I'm more thorough," Buck said.

"Right there's the problem," Tully said. "Too thorough."

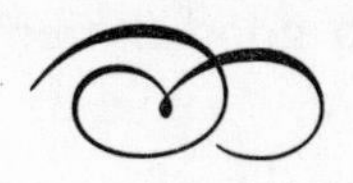

Chapter 29

Batim was out feeding his chickens, which came rushing in to him from all sides. He had one arm around a bucket and was scooping up handfuls of grain from it to scatter about the ground. Tully got out of the Explorer and moseyed over to the old man.

"Those must be what they call free-range chickens," he said.

"That they are, Bo. Can't beat 'em, fried, roasted or boiled with noodles or dumplings. Eggs is mighty good too."

"Must be a chore finding the eggs, though."

"Nope. They go to the henhouse to lay their eggs. Got a few rebels who hide their nests, but most of them are pretty thoughtful. What can I do you for?"

"Oh, I just thought I'd stop by and apologize for flattening Lister the way I did. My nerves have been a bit frayed."

"No need to apologize. Lister needs a good flattening. What did you really stop by for?"

Tully laughed. "I thought maybe you could give me a little help with these murders."

"Be glad to, particularly since you stopped talking about it on the radio. I get myself an expensive scanner and then all the cops stop using the radio. So you got any idea who done it?"

"Not really. Naturally, I got you and the boys on my short list."

"I appreciate that, Bo. I'd be offended if you didn't. But the truth is we didn't have anything to do with it."

"I've just been wondering if you know anything about what Vern Littlefield has been up to lately?"

"You think Vern might have kilt those fellas!" Batim burst out in a cackling laugh.

"No, I don't think Vern killed them. I just thought you might know something, and that for once in your life you might be of a little help to the law."

"I appreciate that, Bo, I really do. But Vern Littlefield and me ain't exactly buddies. He has been acting a little strange, though. That expensive bull of his, for example. It jumps the fence onto my property and he don't even bother to come over and get it. Now the dang beast has run off again. Probably it's halfway to Denver by now."

"I bet it is."

"I sent the boys out to look for it, so they could return it to Littlefield, but you know how boys are."

"I've got a lot more to worry about now than Littlefield's bull. Or yours either, for that matter. When was the last time you talked to Vern?"

"I don't think we've actually talked since about 1956, but I did say howdy to him a week or so ago. He had those city folks with him."

"What did the city folk look like?"

"Two guys in their mid-thirties or so, maybe forty. Vern's apparently got some business going with them. They live out at his ranch."

"Yes, probably the same two I met at his house the other day."

"I expect so." Batim threw another handful of grain out to the chickens.

"I hear your boys are doing pretty well for themselves."

"How's that?"

"They've got more money than usual."

"Shoot, I'd have more money, too, if I lived off my pa all the time. The boys drive off in one of my pickups occasionally. Maybe they're robbing banks. They're out most every night, but they was home the night those fellas got killed. I don't know what they do when they're out. They get cross if I ask too many questions, and it don't pay to get them two fellas riled. You want to arrest them, Bo, be my guest. You'd be doing me a favor."

"It isn't against the law to be mean and nasty. I wish it was, but it isn't."

"You want to take a look around, help yourself."

"I don't think so. Besides, I thought the boys were away."

"Yup, they is. They took my cattle truck. I guess they figured that if they found the bull, they could haul it back to Vern."

"They're such good boys."

"Ain't they?"

"By the way, do you happen to have any ATVs?"

"Of course I do. Got three four-wheelers. Everybody in Blight County has an ATV, I imagine. We use 'em for hunting and things like that. Why, you interested in buying one? I could let you have it real cheap. Hardly been used."

"Sorry, not today, Batim. I've been thinking I should get one, though, just for show. Blight County folks have been looking at me a little odd lately, and I imagine that's why, my not having an ATV."

"It's more likely them pitchers you paint."

"That, too."

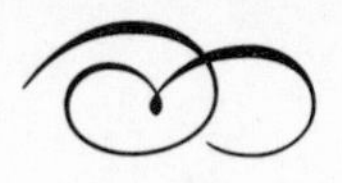

Chapter 30

Tully got to Dave's House of Fry a little before noon. Dave was seated with Pap and Buck at the usual table.

"What's good?" Tully said as he walked up.

"Everything," Dave said. "Business gets any better I may give up on my casino idea."

"I'd recommend the chicken-fried steak again," Pap said. "It'll probably kill you but not right away."

Deedee came over to take his order. "Thanks for what you did the other day, Sheriff. That was nice."

"Anytime, Deedee."

"You're a real gentleman, Bo. If there's anything I can ever do for you, just let me know, okay?"

"Sure," Tully said. "For right now, though, how about bringing me anything but one of those chicken-fried steaks?"

"How about a fried chicken breast?"

"Perfect."

"The cook fries them in half grease, half butter."

"Sounds wonderful."

"It will be on the house, too."

"Thanks a lot, Deedee!" Dave said. "Now I got my waitresses giving away food. No wonder the place is packed."

Tully smiled. "I appreciate Deedee's generosity, but you can put all our meals on the county tab."

"Good," Dave said. "I planned to, anyway."

Pap and Buck were digging into their chicken-frieds with all the gusto of persons on the brink of starvation. Tully studied them silently for a few moments. When he looked up, Dave was watching him and smiling.

"You should feed these boys more often, Bo."

"I suppose," Tully said, "but I'd kind of like to lean them down a bit."

"Ha!" Pap said. "I weigh exactly the same as I did in high school—one sixty-five."

They looked at Buck. He shook his head in refusal to comment on his weight.

Pap wiped his mouth with a napkin. "You ever hear anything from Paul Cooper at Central Electric, Bo? Besides fishing?"

"Yeah, I got some interesting information. Back during one of the country's fuel shortages—I think it was back in the seventies—Congress passed a law that said the electric utility companies had to buy any power produced by private dams, solar panels, windmill farms and whatever. When Vern and his dad heard that, they went out and dammed up Last Hope Creek, one of half a dozen streams that run down out of the Hoodoos and through their property. He hooked up a generator—

don't ask me how, but Vern can do practically anything mechanical—and started selling electricity."

"I guess it didn't pan out for him," Dave said.

"Oh, he has had some good years," Bo said. "In a normal year, with the usual amount of rain and snow, he could make a hundred thousand off the dam."

Buck almost choked on his last mouthful of chicken-fried steak. "A hundred thousand!"

"Sounds like a lot to us poor working stiffs, doesn't it, Buck? But to Vern it was little more than a hobby."

"Yeah," Pap said, "I expect any year he didn't take in at least half a million on the ranch, he was slipping farther down the drain."

"Well, maybe he'll do better on his grapes and winery," Buck said. "At least grapes don't eat."

"Or jump fences," Tully added.

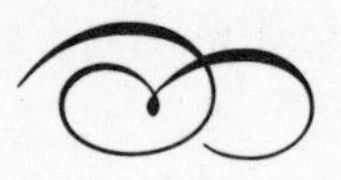

Chapter 31

As they were leaving the restaurant, Tully pulled Dave aside. "I need your services again."

"Same rate of pay?"

"Yeah."

"I may have to open that casino after all."

"See, Dave, I've got this theory that the three dead guys were set up by someone riding in the right rear seat. When the car came up to the berm, one shooter opened up on the front seat. The second shooter hesitated a couple of seconds to let the person in the right rear seat jump out. That hesitation gave Holt, the fellow who made it to Batim's fence, time enough to get out the left rear door. He had his gun out and was shooting wildly. That pool of blood we found back in the woods could mean he may have hit somebody standing back there, maybe not another shooter but an observer. I've got a bad feeling that person was Vern Littlefield. He supposedly went off to his elk camp that night, but I suspect he didn't."

Dave peeled the foil off a stick of Doublemint gum, wadded it up, poked it into his mouth and began to chew. "Cindy had me go up to Vern's hunting camp and look for him, but all I found was his pickup truck. No Vern. There weren't any signs he had even been there. I did have a problem figuring out how Holt could have got out of the car alive with all those bullets ripping through it. But you're saying the rear seat wasn't shot up until Holt was out of the car?"

"That's what I'm saying. We didn't find any shell casings from Holt's gun. So maybe he was using a revolver. Or maybe one of the shooters picked up the casings afterwards. I suspect it was just a matter of chance his random shooting connected with the person in the woods. But what I want you to do is go out to the scene and see if you can find any trees he might have hit. Maybe we can retrieve some of the slugs. If we do, that will help prove my theory."

"Phew!" Dave said. "This is a tough one. A bullet in a tree!"

"Do what you can."

"So where do you want to meet? You could have supper back at the restaurant?"

"No, I've brought some steaks and potatoes and stuff, and we're going to camp out up along the river. You're welcome to join us. I suspect there will be some sipping of whiskey around the campfire."

"Sounds good. But I don't think my old back is up to

sleeping on the ground. What do Pap and Buck think of your little plan?"

"I haven't told them."

"I didn't think so."

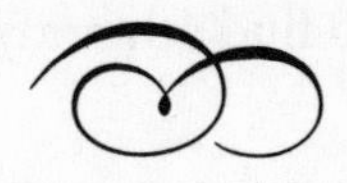

Chapter 32

"We're gonna do what?" Pap shouted.

They were sitting around in chairs back at Ed's gas station. Ed was out front servicing a car.

"I knew you'd like it," Tully said.

"Nights get down to freezing," Buck said.

"I've got some big tarps, three good sleeping bags and a bunch of food in the back of my rig," Tully said. "Plus a fifth of Bushmills to keep us warm. Of course, we could always go stay at the hotel."

"I ain't never going back to that hotel," Buck said. "I don't care what nobody says, the place is haunted."

Pap started rolling himself a cigarette. "You ever figure out who you jumped in the hotel, Bo?"

"Not for sure. I think it was Lem Scragg, though."

Pap paused in the act of licking his cigarette paper. "Lem Scragg! What would he be up there for? Figuring on killing us?"

"I don't think so. He seemed startled to find anybody else in the hotel."

"How about all the ghosts I saw coming down from the cemetery?" Buck said. "How about them?"

"There weren't any ghosts!" Tully said. "You dreamed them!"

"They looked real enough to me. Gives me the creeps just thinking about 'em."

Ed came in wiping his hands on a rag. "What secrets you boys passing behind my back?"

"No secrets," Bo said. "I was just telling Pap and Buck my plan for us to camp out up along the river."

"Getting mighty cold these nights for camping out," Ed said.

"You hear that, Bo?" Buck said. "Even Ed thinks it's too cold to be camping out."

"You ever see such a bunch of pantywaists in your life, Ed? No, we're going to camp out, and that's the end of it."

"You change your mind, Sheriff, I think me and my wife could manage to put you up at the house."

"Appreciate the offer, Ed, but the fellas and I are going to camp out. I don't want to drag you any further into this investigation than is necessary."

"May already be too late, Bo. This station used to be the main communication center for Famine. Now all the gossip has suddenly all dried up. I haven't picked up a single juicy rumor all week. Maybe it's just my imagination, but it seems like the whole town is afraid something real bad is about to happen."

"Something real bad has already happened," Tully said. "We've got three men shot to death."

Pap lit his cigarette. "You know, that was my impression, too, while Buck and me was out canvassing the town." He picked a speck of tobacco off his tongue. "It seemed as if these people were scared to death of something, afraid anything they might say could get them involved in whatever this is. We didn't find a single person who claimed to know anything, did we, Buck?"

"Nope. They seemed real nervous, too. But, anyway, I think we should reconsider Ed's offer to put us up for the night."

"Forget it!" Tully said. "You're camping out!"

Chapter 33

Tully drove out onto a wooded bluff half a mile from the highway. The bluff overlooked the river. Buck pulled in behind him. Down below, the Blight River made a broad turn, cottonwoods lining a steep bank on the far side, a sandy beach protruding into the river on the near side. Tully had camped on the bluff as a teenager, and it wasn't one of his fonder memories. It didn't look as if anyone had camped there since.

"Here's the program," he told Pap and Buck as they climbed out of the other Explorer. "Pap, you build us a fire pit with some rocks. Buck, you get us a night's supply of firewood, and I'll unload the camp gear."

Pap and Buck went to work with a distinct lack of enthusiasm, but soon they had the camp set up and the fire crackling away. Tully and Buck moved a couple of log sections over to the fire for seats.

"So what's for supper?" Buck asked. "It better be good."

"It is good," Tully said. "Nothing better. Rib steak grilled over an open fire. Also, I'm slicing up potatoes, alternating the potato slices with onion slices, putting a dollop of butter on each and wrapping each up in foil to roast."

"Reminds me of Boy Scouts," Buck said.

"You sure those sleeping bags are warm enough for out here?" Pap said, hunching down into his mackinaw.

"Supposed to be good all the way down to twenty below."

"Might serve. Where'd you get them, anyway?"

"County bought them. Supposed to be part of the search-and-rescue operation I started."

"Rescued anybody yet?"

"One crabby old fellow who claimed he wasn't lost, just spending the night out in the snow. We hauled him in, and he groused every inch of the way. Turned out the old nut often spent nights out there in the snow, but it was good practice for us anyway."

"I hear it's better to stay lost than to have Blight County Search and Rescue find you," Pap said.

"Some of the boys are a little wild," Tully said. "But all in all I think it's better for folks to be found."

Buck spread out the tarps on three sides of the fire and started unrolling a sleeping bag on each. "These the same bags we used last night?" Pap said.

"Yeah, first time they were used. My crew of search-and-rescuers aren't dedicated enough to spend a night out when they're looking for someone."

Pap laughed. "You ever have to search for somebody, it'll probably be for Buck."

"That's all you know, Pap," Buck said. "I've been running around these mountains my whole life and ain't never been lost once."

Darkness had slipped up out of the valley below. Tully was cooking the steak on a hand-held grill, using one of his leather gloves for a pot holder. He could no longer see the color of the steak, so he had Buck grab him a flashlight out of the Explorer. He shined the light on the grill and realized the flashlight had arrived just in time. He put on his other glove, grabbed the foil packages one by one and dropped them on the aluminum plates being held out to him by Buck and Pap.

"Smells pretty good," Pap said, opening his package. "Didn't know you could cook so good, Bo."

"Only over an open fire."

"So what's for dessert?" Buck asked, forking a chunk of steak into his mouth.

"Bushmills."

After supper they sat around poking the fire with sticks and sipping whiskey. It was times like this Tully wished he had taken up pipe smoking, maybe a nice corncob. Ginger had always been dead set against his smoking anything, even the occasional cigar. "You'll live a whole lot longer, Bo," she had said. So far he had outlived Ginger by nearly ten years.

Bit by bit the fire died down. Tully threw on a couple more logs, and it blazed up again. Several cars full of high school kids pulled in next to the beach down below. They howled and yelled and played their music at deafening levels until almost midnight. Tully was about ready to drive down and send them all home, when he heard someone scrambling up through the brush from below. Two teenage girls stumbled out on top of the bluff. They walked over and looked down at Pap in his sleeping bag.

"We're cold," one of them said.

"Freezing," said the other.

"Unzip that sleeping bag, old man, and let us slip in beside you and get warm."

"Yeah, mister, let us get warmed up a bit."

Tully had had enough. "You girls get away from that old man and leave him alone. Scat out of here before I arrest the whole bunch of you."

The girls looked over and saw the light bars on the Explorers. They ran off down the bluff screaming and giggling. Suddenly, down below, the music stopped and car engines roared to life. Silence at long last settled back over the valley.

Then out of the darkness Pap growled, "Won't you ever learn to mind your own business, Bo?"

Chapter 34

By early morning, it was snowing. Buck awoke Pap and Tully by yelling one of his ten-letter obscenities.

Tully peeked out from under his blue plastic tarp, half of which, like Buck and Pap, he had folded over his sleeping bag. He shuddered. "At least you were warm and cozy all night in your twenty-below sleeping bag, Buck."

Pap groaned. "I'm too old for this. I need something between me and the hard, cold ground. Like a couple floors of a nice hotel."

Tully thought he should respond to the comment with a laugh, but wasn't up to it. He ached all over. Too bad Pap and Buck hadn't had enough sense between them to talk him out of this stupid idea.

"Okay, okay, stop complaining," Tully told them. "I'll take you to the House of Fry for breakfast."

"You call that a bribe?" Pap said. "The House of Fry is killing me."

"Sounds good to me," Buck said.

Already the snow was turning to rain. It would be piling up in the mountains, though. Tully thought of the Cliff kid. If the snow didn't bring him down, he would have to go get him. If Vern Littlefield was up there chasing elk, it would bring him down, too.

They rolled up the sleeping bags and tossed them in the back of Tully's Explorer. Then they shook as much rain off the blue tarps as they could and folded them up and stashed them away. The cooler still contained half a bottle of Bushmills, several cans of soda and most of the ice. He could have forgotten the ice.

There was always something particularly miserable about breaking camp in the rain. Perhaps for the first time in his life, Tully looked forward to the warmth and roar of talk and laughter at the House of Fry. And the smell of hot grease.

Pap rode with him back to the restaurant, working most of the time on rolling himself a cigarette. "Hands are so dang cold from camping out I can't make my fingers work right."

"Stop complaining," Tully said.

"My birthday was several days ago. Are we still celebrating?"

"Sure, doesn't it feel like it? I sometimes forget that you've turned into a senior citizen."

"I hate being called that. Besides, I'm as good as I ever was. Better than you by far."

"What does that mean?"

"You want me to give you a for-instance? How about women? If you knew as much about women as I do, you wouldn't be forever having so many problems with them."

"Let me see if I remember this correctly. I seem to recall a fellow a number of years ago who ran naked out the back door of a house and climbed over a board fence while the lady of the house stood in the doorway and shot at him with his own thirty-eight revolver."

"I seem to recall a situation vaguely similar," Pap said, smiling. "I think the lady's name was Mo. For Maureen. She was one terrific gal, as I recall, and a wonderful shot, too. She grazed me across the ribs with one round. Stung like heck. If she hadn't been such a good shot, she might have killed me."

"Maybe Mo was a bad shot," Tully said. "Did you ever think of that?"

"Nope, I never did."

All the trees around Dave's House of Fry dripped with melting snow as Tully pulled into the parking lot. Oddly, the parking lot was nearly empty.

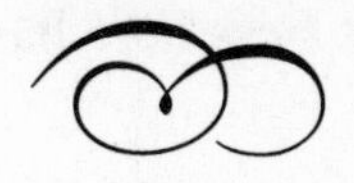

Chapter 35

They slid into a booth at the House of Fry.

"Uh-oh," said Tully. "No Deedee today. Not here to fuss over old codgers."

"You must think I'm as woman-starved as you," Pap said. "Fact is, I can take them or leave them alone."

"Is that your secret?" Buck said.

"Mind your own business," Pap said. "Besides, I can't be giving pointers to a young fella like you. Bo would probably arrest me."

"I probably would," Tully said.

They ordered the pancakes, with sides of eggs, bacon and hash browns.

"One or two pancakes?" the waitress said.

"Two, of course," Pap said. "How come you always ask?"

"Dave makes us ask, because the pancakes are so big. He doesn't like to waste food, even if the customer is paying for it."

"It won't be wasted," Buck said. "The boss here has had us camping out for a week and we're starving."

"Camping out? In this weather? The sheriff must be a lot meaner than I've heard." She gave Tully a big smile.

He checked her out more thoroughly. Not bad. A bit plumper than Deedee, but not bad. Probably already in love with him. He gave her his warm look and was thinking of something to say when Dave walked over and slid into the booth.

"You okay, Bo?" he said.

"Yes, I'm okay!"

"Don't get sore. You just looked a little odd there for a moment."

"Did you do what I asked you to do?" Tully said.

"Don't I always?"

"I guess. Find anything?"

"As a matter of fact, I did. All right to share it with these two galoots?"

"Yeah, they're a couple of blabbermouths, but go ahead."

"I checked every tree that might have been hit and found one bullet hole. I dug it out with my knife. Don't worry, I was careful not to scratch it." He handed Tully the bullet, wrapped up in a handkerchief. "It looks to me like a forty-five caliber."

"You find any shell casings?"

"Not a one. The ambushers must have picked them up, but you'd think they would have missed at least one."

Tully unwrapped the handkerchief and looked at the

slug. "Could be a forty-five, all right," he said. "My theory gets better all the time."

"At least it would if we had Holt's gun," Pap said.

"That is a problem. But if someone from around here found it, he probably kept it. My bet would be it was the fellow that killed Holt, one of the two ambushers at the car."

"I've got another question for you, Dave," Tully said. "That new waitress of yours, she married?"

"Bo has a hard time keeping his mind on criminal activity," Pap said.

"You mean like you, Pap, back when you were sheriff?" Dave said.

"As I recall, you were a bit of a scoundrel yourself. And don't think for a minute I've taken you off my list of suspects, Dave. It would be a perfect setup for you. Here we've got you doing our tracking for us and looking for bullets, hanging out on the law side of this investigation, you thinking we'd never suspect you."

"Interesting idea, Pap," Tully said. "What do you have to say about that, Dave?"

Dave thought for a moment. "I must have a good alibi. If I don't I'll think of one pretty quick." Dave scratched his chin. "Let's see, I had to be somewhere. What's on the TV that night? Oh yeah, I remember now. I was home in bed by midnight. My wife will probably attest to that. She's been kind of ornery lately, but I think she will. Is that good enough?"

"Good enough for me," Tully said. "I may still have use for a good tracker. After that, I'm not so sure. By the way, I've got another little job for you."

"Why am I so lucky?"

"Beats me. I want you to go up to the Last Hope Mine and have a close look around. You can do it in the daytime."

"What am I looking for?"

"I'm not sure, but you'll know it when you find it."

"Thanks. It's always easier to find something when you're specific like that."

Pap shook his head. "I don't think it's a good idea to dismiss Dave as a suspect. If you arrested him right now, Bo, we could all go home."

Buck suddenly stopped eating and looked up from his plate.

"What is it, Buck?" Tully said.

"I was just thinking," Buck said.

"I told you to stop doing that," Pap said.

"You know it was a moonlit night when those fellas was hit," Buck said.

"Right," Tully said. "So what's your point, Buck?"

"The fella after Holt, he wouldn't have wanted to use a flashlight, at least until he found Holt's gun, if he did find it. So he had to be a good tracker himself, to follow Holt only by moonlight."

Everybody stopped eating and stared at Buck.

"You know what, Buck," Tully said. "If you keep coming up with stuff like this, I might have to give you a promotion. There aren't that many trackers around these days."

Buck went back to his pancakes. "I thought you might want to think about a promotion," he said.

"It's true," Pap said. "We probably do need to look for a tracker."

Tully said, "I doubt either of those two fellows staying at Littlefield's place is a tracker, seeing as how they're both from L.A. Shooters maybe, but not trackers."

Pap looked at Dave. "A local boy, no doubt."

"Maybe I'll check with Madeline," Dave said. "Just to make sure she supports my alibi."

Tully looked around at all the empty booths and tables. "Kind of slim pickings this morning, ain't it, Dave?"

"To tell you the truth, it's about as bad as I've ever seen it. Must be something going on."

"Something that could scare a whole town?" Pap said.

"Yeah," Dave said. "Maybe you fellas should stop eating here all the time. Gives the place a bad name."

Chapter 36

After breakfast, Tully and Pap stopped by Ed's station, to check the gossip circuit.

"It's very strange," Ed said. "Nobody is talking much. It's like there's some big secret nobody wants to reveal."

"You mean the residents of Famine know something you don't?"

"Seems like it. I usually know what's going on, but this silence beats the heck out of me. It can't be those three fellows that got themselves killed. Folks talked that to pieces. But ever since you and Pap showed up and started asking questions, Bo, the whole town seems to have stopped talking. People are nervous."

"Got any idea what would make them nervous?" Tully asked.

"Nothing I know about. Everybody turns pretty nervous when Vern Littlefield gets in an uproar. He can be pretty mean and take it out on most anybody he feels like. But as far as I know, he hasn't bothered anybody lately."

"I've known him to get in a bit of a snit, all right," Tully said.

"Snit isn't exactly the right word," Pap said. "Vern can get pretty darn mean. But he isn't half as mean as his old man. Not only was Cruise Littlefield mean, he was smart, too. As far as I can tell, Vern inherited only the mean part and not all of that."

"He may not be all that smart, but he sure has a grip on this town," Ed said. "For one thing, he owns most all the houses in it. One by one he's bought them up over the years and then rents them out."

Tully selected a candy bar from a display on the counter and peeled the wrapper back. He dug in his pocket, took out a quarter and placed it on the counter. "How do folks around here survive, anyway?"

"They do as little as possible," Ed said. "A few of them still trap in the winter, but there's not much of a market for furs anymore. Some of them work in the woods, but there's not much logging either. Quite a few old folks get by on their Social Security. One thing, it doesn't cost a whole lot to live in Famine."

Tully bit off a chunk from his candy bar. It didn't taste as if it was more than five years old.

Pap looked at him and shook his head. "I thought you just ate a two-pancake breakfast at the House of Fry."

"I'm still a growing boy," Tully said. "By the way, Ed, you run the station all by yourself?"

"Practically. I have old Lucas fix tires for me sometimes. I wouldn't trust him with the keys to the gas pumps, though."

"I don't recall seeing anyone else around," Tully said.

"He's a big old guy. Wears a stupid cap with the ear-muffs. As far as I know, he even sleeps in the ratty thing."

"Stupid cap," Tully said. "I didn't know caps had IQs." He pointed out the side window to a small yellow school bus parked in the lot next to the station. "You drive the school bus, too, Ed?"

"Naw, that belongs to Lucas. That's why I don't trust him with the keys to the gas pumps. He'd be filling that bus up all the time. It's all rusted out, but he's got some idea he can turn it into a camper. He probably figures he can then turn himself into a hippy."

"Shucks," Tully said, "I've thought about doing that myself. Just never found a school bus." He turned to Pap. "Well, maybe we'll drive out to the Littlefields' and see if Vern has put in an appearance yet."

"You think Littlefield might be involved with these killings?" Ed said.

"Yep, one way or another. I think I've got all the pieces now. I just need to put them together."

"You want to look over that pretty wife of his again," Pap said.

"That, too."

"Maybe I'll go back to Blight City with Buck," Pap said.

"Oh, you might as well go with me. Otherwise my lungs will miss the cigarette smoke. I'll only be a minute at the Littlefields'. Then I'm headed into Blight. Besides, it isn't as if you have any important business to attend to."

"That's all you know, Bo. I've got a woman coming in to see about a housekeeping job." He shoved himself up out of the chair and started for the door.

"I pity that poor desperate soul," Tully said.

He could tell that the night of camping had taken a lot out of the old man. For that matter, it had taken a lot out of him.

"You hear anything that's going on here, absolutely anything, you let me know, okay, Ed?" he said. "I'll be back in Blight for a few days. A sheriff can't spend all his time on interesting stuff like murder."

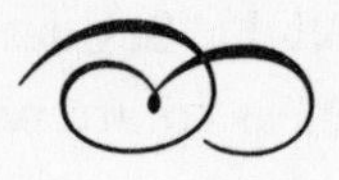

Chapter 37

They turned into a farm road directly out from the Littlefield house. Tully pulled up behind some trees.

"What now?" Pap said.

Bo swept his field glasses back and forth, looking for any activity. "Just want to check out a few things."

Pap sighed and leaned his head against his window. Soon he began to snore. Half an hour later, he sat up, startled. "What's wrong?"

"Nothing is wrong. I just want to look over the Littlefield place for a while."

"We could be back in Blight by now."

"What do you care, Pap? You've been sleeping the whole time, anyway."

"Yeah, I've got a knot in my neck big as a baseball to show for it, too. Let's go."

"I've got to stop by the Littlefields' first."

Pap muttered a four-letter obscenity.

They drove up in front of the Littlefield house. Pap stayed in the Explorer while Tully got out and rang the doorbell. Cindy Littlefield opened the door.

"Oh, hi," she said, startled, as if she had been expecting someone else.

"Hi," said Tully.

Behind her in the living room he could see the lady from the General Store. She started to get up and perhaps out of sight, but it was too late. She knew Tully had already seen her. Giving a hopeless shrug, she sank back down into the easy chair. She was holding a coffee cup. Another cup, probably Cindy's, sat on the coffee table.

Tully raised his hand in greeting.

The lady, obviously embarrassed, raised hers back.

"You know my sister?" Cindy said.

"Your sister?" Tully said. "Yes, we met at the General Store."

"Oh, I hadn't heard. What can I do for you, Sheriff?"

"Just checking to see if Vern made it back from his elk hunt."

"Not yet. But he did drive up to a place where his cell phone would work. He called last night."

"He did? So everything is all right?"

"Yes, Vern's fine. He said he would be up in the mountains for another couple of days."

"That's good news. Any luck?"

"I'm afraid not. But he still has hopes."

"About what time did you talk to him?"

"Oh, I didn't. He called Mitchell. I guess he had

some things he wanted Bob to take care of. Bob passed the message on to me."

"Oh. By the way, are Mitchell and Kincaid around? I'd like to talk with them."

"They're on the ranch, but I don't know where. They live in the other house over there. Nothing like first-class accommodations for your employees. You're welcome to come in and wait. I imagine they'll be coming in soon."

"I don't have time right now, but I do have a question. The one called Harry Kincaid? Was he, by any chance, raised around here? For some reason he looks familiar to me."

"You know he's from Los Angeles?"

"Yes, that's why I wonder why he looks familiar."

"He has several brothers who live around here. Maybe you're thinking of one of them. The Kincaids live way back in the hills. His father was a trapper, probably still is. Harry did some trapping, too, but I guess the father was pretty fierce and mean and a little crazy. So Harry took off for L.A. when he was still a kid. That's all I know about him."

"It's probably just my imagination. Someone looks familiar to me, I can't get him out of my head. Not too bad for a lawman, I suppose, but it gets to be a nuisance. Sorry to have bothered you. If Vern shows up, have him give me a call, will you? I'll probably be at home the next couple of days, so have him call me there. You have a pencil and paper, I'll give you the number."

"I'll be right back," Cindy said.

She walked back into the house, apparently toward the office. Tully and the woman from the General Store stared at each other. Suddenly the woman burst out laughing, got up and walked over to Tully. She was trim and attractive, wearing a gray cardigan sweater over a white blouse and jeans.

She held out her hand. "I'm Dana Cassidy."

"Hi," Tully said. "I'm Bo Tully. I guess the job in Boise didn't work out."

"Actually, there was no job in Boise. I've been hired to cook for the Littlefields and their crew."

"They don't have much of a crew anymore."

"Actually, I'm not that great of a cook, but I'm a whole lot better than Cindy. I've known Bob Mitchell and Vern Littlefield for a long time. Vern and the Littlefields are helping me over kind of a rough patch. Cindy and I keep each other company." She sighed, shook her head and laughed. It was a nice laugh. "I don't know why I lied to you at the store. I guess it's just a habit when I'm talking to strangers. You don't have to stand there in the doorway, Sheriff. Come in and sit down."

"Sorry, but I can't. That's my father waiting in the car. He just turned seventy-five and is terribly cranky about it."

Cindy Littlefield returned with a pad and pen, and he gave her his home number.

"By the way, Ms. Cassidy," he said, "I appreciate your recommendation on Danielle Steel."

"You found a book you liked?"

"I did, indeed."

She laughed. "You don't seem the type."

"Really?" he said. "Well, I loved the book." He was about to try his warm look on her, but then thought better of it.

Pap stuck his head out the window of the Explorer and yelled. "Bo, get over here! Fast! We just got a call on the radio!"

"Sorry, gotta go. If Vern calls again, tell him I have to talk to him right away. Very important."

"Is it about those people who were killed?"

"I can't discuss it. Please have Vern give me a call." Tully turned and ran back to the car.

"For heaven's sake, Pap, what is it?"

"It just came over the radio! An officer's down out on Highway 95! I think it's Buck."

He took out his cell phone and called Daisy.

"Yes, it's Buck!" she told him. "Someone shot through his windshield right before a turn. Buck didn't make the turn."

"Is he . . ."

"No, not yet, anyway. He got broken glass sprayed in his face and a bunch of cuts from that. The bullet hit him in the right shoulder but didn't go through his vest. He got banged up, too, from going off the road and flipping over. That's the info from the State Police. The ambulance is on its way out there now."

"So he's going to be . . ."

"I don't know. The patrolman didn't think his injuries were fatal."

"Pap and I are on our way into Blight City right now. We'll stop by the hospital on our way in."

As he wheeled the Explorer around to head out the driveway, Tully noticed the two women still standing on the porch, watching.

"I don't know why anyone would shoot Buck," Pap said.

Tully tugged hard on the corner of his mustache. "That's what I was thinking."

Chapter 38

At the accident scene, they could see Buck's Explorer lying on its top in tall grass off to the side of the highway and on the outside edge of the curve. A state patrolman was directing traffic around a Blight City wrecker that blocked one lane.

Tully walked over to the patrolman. "What happened, Bill?"

"Buck took a bullet through his windshield, sprayed glass all over his face and hit him on the right shoulder. I think most of the damage was done when he went off the road."

"Any idea where the shooter was?"

The patrolman pointed up the hill. "I'm out here all by myself and haven't had a chance to look around. I think he had to be up there, somewhere in direct line with the road."

A car in the line behind them began to honk irritably.

"I should rip out that jerk's horn wires," Tully said.

"I wish you would," said the patrolman.

"Anyway, Pap and I are going to look at Buck's vehicle before it gets towed."

Tully drove around the curve and found a place to park. He and Pap walked back along the highway and climbed down to the wreck. The two wrecker men were arranging straps to roll the Explorer back onto its wheels.

"Hold up a second," Tully told them. "We need to have a look at this."

One of the wrecker men shrugged and dug out his pipe and began to fill it from a leather tobacco pouch. His partner finished fastening a cable to the vehicle, then sat down on a rock.

Tully got on his knees and looked into the front seat.

"Not too much blood," he told Pap. "The medics must have got to him right away."

One of the wrecker men walked over and stood above him, gesturing with his pipe. "He crawled out the passenger-side window. It had all the glass knocked out of it. There's more blood over there but not too much, I guess."

"Was Buck gone when you got here?"

"Yep. The ambulance was just pulling away. We're only about twenty minutes from the hospital, so they did get to him pretty fast. A motorist called the wreck in on a cell phone."

Tully studied the shattered windshield. "Whoever shot him meant to kill him. A few inches to the left and it would have been a head shot."

"Bad business," said the wrecker man.

Tully got back to his feet. "Wait for me in the car, Pap," he said. "I'm going to climb up the hill and see if I can find the place the shot came from."

"Suits me."

Tully scrambled up the bank and crossed the highway.

Cars were now backed up twice as far, the patrolman standing in the middle of the curve, directing cars around him in the single lane. Tully pulled himself up the hillside by grabbing small trees and branches. Once he reached the woods, the ground leveled out slightly and he was able to climb standing up. Thirty feet up he found a spot where the shooter had sat, his rifle resting on a stout tree limb directly in line with the highway. He had broken off some tiny branches to make a clear rest for the rifle. Tully closed one eye and aimed an imaginary gun at one of the cars in line down below. It would have been an easy shot, the car coming at him head-on. The shooter had to know it was a Blight County Sheriff's Department car. As he had hoped, a shell casing lay on the ground next to the base of the tree. Either the shooter was careless or stupid. Tully hoped the latter.

He picked the casing up with his pen, put it in his pocket and then climbed farther up the hill. The shooter certainly wouldn't have walked to this place, he thought. A couple dozen yards up the hill, he came to an old logging road. It was covered with pine needles too thick to allow a foot to make an impression. He walked down the road and soon came to a rotten tree that had fallen across it. He climbed over the tree. There were some scuff marks where some of the loose bark had been kicked away. There were also impressions of tires on the lower side of the log. The tires were set close together. The shooter had arrived and left by ATV. He would get Lurch up here to make impressions of the tracks.

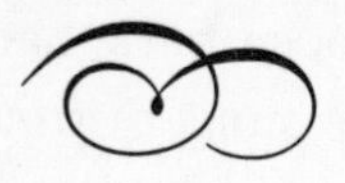

Chapter 39

It was ten o'clock at night. Tully and Pap had talked to the doctor who had treated Buck. "Coming through the windshield glass pretty well messed up the slug," he said. "It was stuck in Buck's vest. I've got it in my office. You can pick it up there."

"Thanks," Tully said.

A nurse told them Buck was awake but heavily medicated and that they weren't to stay long.

Buck seemed glad to see them. He smiled weakly. His massive chest was wrapped in bandages and his right arm was in a cast. The entire right side of his head was also covered with bandages, leaving only his left eye to blink at them.

"How you doing, Buck?" Pap said.

"Okay," Buck said. "After that camping out, I needed a vacation, anyway."

"I think you may have taken a bullet intended for me," Tully told him.

"That's about what I figure," Buck said. "Who would want to shoot me?"

"I don't suppose you have any idea who shot you," Tully said.

"Naw. I did see a flash of light up on the hillside. I must be getting jumpy, because for some reason I thought of sun reflecting off a scope. I would have swerved left and back until I got around the curve, but a car was coming in the other lane. Then there was a terrific explosion, the shot hitting the windshield, I guess. The next thing I remember I was laying on some grass alongside the Explorer. And there was some people standing around me, and some guy was yelling, 'Don't touch him, don't touch him.'"

"You get a look at any of those people?" Tully asked.

"No, I thought I might be blind. I had some cuts in my forehead and the blood was running down in my eyes. Couldn't see a thing."

"You'll have some good-looking scars, anyway," Pap said. "No point in having scars people can't see. I have a few of those myself."

"I'll bet you do," Buck said. He laughed and then winced.

Tully said, "We've got a couple of your pretty nurses telling us to leave you alone, that you need your rest, so we'd better leave."

"Pretty nurses? I guess I haven't seen them yet."

"Take it easy, Buck," Pap said. "And give the nurses a hard time."

"You bet," Buck said.

Tully and Pap rode the elevator back to the lobby.

There were three chrome coffee thermoses on a table near a couch. Tully walked over and flopped back on the couch.

"Pour me a cup, will you?" he said to Pap.

Pap got two foam cups out of a packet next to the thermoses and pumped out two coffees.

"Cream and sugar?"

"How does it taste?"

Pap took a sip. "Like you'd expect hospital coffee to taste."

"In that case, dump in some of the white stuff."

Pap dumped in some white stuff and stirred it with a little stick. He handed the cup to Tully. He didn't put any of the white stuff in his own coffee, but tore open two packs of sugar and dumped them in.

Pap sat down on the couch next to Tully. "I hope you're not conking out on me, Bo."

"I'm not conking out. It just upsets me that one of my men got hurt."

"Upsets me, too," Pap said. "A lot of folks deserve to get shot, but Buck isn't one of them."

"Why would someone shoot Buck? Do you suppose we've got some nut out there randomly shooting cops?"

"Could be, but I don't think so. You know that red Explorer of yours looks exactly like Buck's red Explorer. Except his is cleaner."

"So you think someone mistook Buck for me?"

"That's what I think."

"Who knew we were headed back to Blight City?"

"As far as I know," Pap said, "the only person you

mentioned it in front of was Ed, back at the station. So probably the whole town knew within half an hour."

Tully tugged thoughtfully on the corner of his mustache. "You don't think Ed is involved in this business, do you?"

"I never count out anybody in a murder. The good news is, if that shot was intended for you, somebody must think you're getting pretty close to solving this thing."

"I wish somebody was right," Tully said. "Anyway, as soon as I pick up that slug from the doctor, I've got to stop by the office and check on things there. So I'll probably stay in town tonight. I'm heading back up to Famine the day after tomorrow. You want to come?"

"No. But I will. You aren't smart enough to handle a difficult situation like this all by yourself."

"Thanks."

"You're worrying these murders to death, Bo. Maybe Susan could take your mind off them."

"She probably could do that, all right. Don't know if she would, though. She seems like a very orderly person. I'm pretty much a mess most of the time."

Pap drained the last of his hospital coffee, shuddered slightly and stood up. "Sounds like the perfect combination to me."

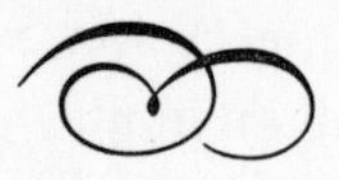

Chapter 40

Tully parked in his reserved space in the parking lot and headed into the courthouse. Some jail inmates were out in the cage playing basketball. They stopped to look at Tully. He looked back. For the first time, they all looked innocent to him. He held up his hand in greeting. Several of them returned the gesture. Those, of course, would be the sociopaths. Normal people remain angry at being put in jail. Still, it was nice to get a polite response for a change. Thank goodness for sociopaths.

Even though it was Sunday, several of his deputies were waiting in the briefing room when he arrived. He had told both Daisy and Eliot that he wanted them to work over the weekend. Neither seemed to view it as a hardship.

"How's Buck?" Deputy Chet Mason asked.

"Fine," Tully told him. "Plus, he gets to spend a few days in a hospital bed with pretty nurses making a fuss over him."

"Sounds good," said Deputy Brian Pugh.

"How come you fellas aren't out hunting for criminals?" Tully asked. "I don't recall reading that criminals take Sunday off."

"Just wondered if you might know why somebody is out there shooting deputies," Mason said.

"Anyone afraid of getting shot can quit right now," Tully said. "The possibility of getting shot comes with the job."

"We know that," said Mason, who seemed to be the spokesman for the group. "It's just that we'd like to know if some nut out there is randomly shooting deputies."

"I'm not sure," Tully said. "But I don't think so. I don't want to have myself quoted in the media about this, but I'm pretty sure Buck was a case of mistaken identity."

"You mean somebody thought Buck was you?" Mason said.

"That's my guess."

"That's a relief," Pugh said.

Tully gave him a look.

Pugh grinned broadly. "Only kidding, Bo."

"Anyway," Tully said, "there's nothing I can tell you now about who shot Buck or why. It's probably got something to do with the mess up in Famine. I don't think you boys have anything to worry about, at least nothing more than you usually worry about. So now I would like you all to hit the pavement. Or your SUV seats."

The deputies trooped out, grousing among themselves. Ah, back to normal, Tully thought.

"You been feeding Wallace?" he said to Daisy.

"Yes, sometimes twice a day, if there's a fly handy. But I hate that spider and he hates me."

"Hold on for a couple more days. We may get this thing in Famine wrapped up soon."

"Really? I sure hope so. It gets lonely around here."

Tully was going through the door of his office. He stopped and looked back at Daisy. "By the way, how are you and Albert getting along?"

"Great."

"That's good."

"Yeah, he moved out a week ago, and there hasn't been a cross word between us since."

"You're getting divorced?"

"Looks that way."

"Sorry I brought it up. Would you get Paul Cooper over at Central Electric on the phone for me? You'll have to reach him at home."

"You bet, Sheriff."

Tully had known Paul Cooper for more than thirty years. He'd been a pretty decent fellow at one time, but then he'd seen the movie *A River Runs Through It*. A day later he was out buying six-hundred-dollar fly rods and the flies and tackle to go with them. He ordered a top-of-the-line fly-fishing vest, hat and waders from Orvis. Suddenly, and for once in his life, Cooper had style. He looked perfect out fishing Henry's Fork. But he was about the worst fisherman Tully had ever seen. He should have taken one of Orvis's fly-fishing clinics, too.

His phone buzzed. Tully sprawled out in his chair

and picked up the receiver. "Paul Cooper on One," Daisy said.

Tully punched the One button.

"How you doing, Paul?"

"Fine, Bo. You?"

"Excellent."

"Does this have anything to do with those murders up in Famine?"

"Can't talk about that. Of course, I could subpoena the info from you if I figured you would put me to all the trouble."

"Tell me again, how big were those cutthroat?"

"About twenty inches, maybe a little more."

"Okay, Bo, tell me what you want to know."

Tully told him.

"You be in your office?" Cooper said.

"Yeah."

"I'll call you right back."

Chapter 41

While he was waiting for Paul Cooper to call him back, Tully wandered out into the briefing room. Herb Eliot was sitting on the edge of Daisy's desk. Daisy was laughing at something he'd said.

"I hate to interrupt, but could I have a few moments of your precious time, Herb?"

"Sure, boss. My place or yours?"

Daisy laughed even harder.

Herb grinned at her. "I'm really on today, aren't I?"

"Yours," Tully growled.

After they'd entered Herb's glassed-in cubicle, Tully closed the door behind them.

"You don't have something going with Daisy, do you, Herb?" he asked.

"What? No, I'm happily married. Let me rephrase that. I'm married. I was just having a little fun with her."

"You know that Daisy and Albert the Awful are separated, getting a divorce?"

"No!"

"It's true. She just told me."

"You want me to cool it, Bo, I'm already cool."

"Okay, Daisy's problem is just between you and me. I don't want it to become briefing-room gossip."

"Not a problem."

"Anyway, the main thing I wanted to talk to you about is I think this thing up in Famine may go down Tuesday night, day after tomorrow."

"Really? I didn't know you were this close."

"Maybe I'm not. But if it does go down Tuesday, I want you and three deputies with me. Pap will be there, too. The deputies should know how to handle guns pretty well."

"Sounds serious. Well, how about Brian Pugh and Chet Mason?"

"Mason is kind of a loudmouth, but I guess this isn't going to involve a lot of talking. Okay, those two and find another good one."

"The new guy, Thorpe, Ernie Thorpe. He's sharp."

"Good. Those three then. You tell them we have serious business and there may be shooting. You shouldn't have to tell them to wear their vests, but tell them anyway. They can bring whatever handguns they prefer. Tell them to keep their traps shut. This means around wives and girlfriends, too. Particularly the girlfriends."

Eliot's phone buzzed. He picked up the receiver.

"Yeah?" He listened, then turned to Tully. "Daisy says your call is on Line One."

"Tell her I'll take it in my office."

He walked back to his office, closed the door. He punched One and picked up. "Paul?"

"Yeah, it's me. I got you the information you wanted, but I think I should make you get that subpoena."

"C'mon, Paul, that's not the Blight way."

"I suppose not. Anyway, here it is. You got a pencil?"

"I don't need a pencil."

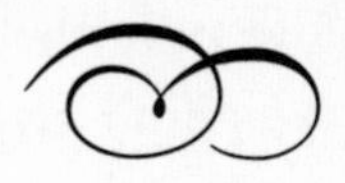

Chapter 42

Tully found Susan in her office. She was frowning as she sorted through a stack of papers. She was wearing her dark-rimmed glasses. She looked very good in glasses.

"How about dinner at my house?" he said.

She took off her glasses and peered up at him. "Your house? You cook?"

"Sure. Sort of."

"Actually, I'm really beat. I wouldn't be much fun."

"Let me be the judge of that," Tully said. "Listen, I'll put you in my big fat easy chair with your feet up on the cassock, and I'll give you a foot massage. Then I'll mix us a pitcher of martinis, with a whole bowl of olives on the side, my special anchovy-stuffed olives. And really good gin. Do you know really good gin?"

"No."

"Good. And then I'll roast us each a grouse. I took two out of the freezer."

"We each get a whole roasted grouse? I've never had grouse before. Where in the world did you find two grouse? Don't tell me you're one of those people who go around shooting little birds?"

"Who, me? No way! I found them badly injured alongside the road and was rushing them to the vet when they expired on the front seat."

Susan smiled slightly. "Okay, as long as you promise you had no part in their murder."

"Cross my heart."

Susan smiled a bit more broadly. "Men are such liars." He could tell she was exhausted.

"Actually," she continued, "it was the martinis that won me over."

"I wish I'd known. You're a lot easier than I expected."

"Your expectations better not go beyond martinis and grouse. And the foot massage."

"I give a great foot massage. What time can I pick you up? As soon as you get done here?"

"I'll never get done here. How about five? Or I can just drive to your place."

"It's impossible to find," he said. "I'll pick you up at five."

On his way back to the office, Tully stopped by the florist's shop at the hospital. He ordered a dozen long-stemmed red roses to be delivered to Buck's hospital room.

"And whom should I say they are from?" the clerk asked.

Tully thought for a moment. "Just write 'From a Secret Admirer.'"

When he got to the office, Herb Eliot was again sitting on the corner of Daisy's desk. "Looks like I have to find more work for you, Herb," he told the undersheriff.

"Just dictating my last will and testament," Eliot said.

"Good. Your family may have need of it."

He walked into his office and stood looking out the window. A wind had come up and there were a few whitecaps on Lake Blight. A boat bobbed about a couple hundred yards offshore. Tully tugged on the corner of his mustache. After a moment, he opened the top drawer of the gray file cabinet next to the window. He took out a pair of binoculars and trained them on the boat. Two people were seated back under the canvas top. He could see only their legs. A fishing rod was in a rod holder on each side of the boat. The boat appeared to be well used. Obviously, the occupants were a couple of fishermen who must have known what they were doing. So why were they trolling there? No one ever caught any fish trolling off the city beach.

"Daisy, get in here," he yelled out the door.

She scurried in, perky as ever. "I don't care what he tells you, Bo, I've been feeding him every day!"

"Who?"

"Wallace."

He had forgotten all about his spider. "Oh, Wallace. Good. But it's not about that. I want you to get somebody up here and have this window painted."

"Paint the window? But that will ruin your view of the lake."

"I know. But get it painted anyway."

"Are you afraid somebody might take a shot at you through the window?"

"It's possible."

"But they would have to be in a boat out in the lake in order to hit this window. It would be a really difficult shot even then, bobbing around in a boat."

Tully turned and looked at her.

"Okay," she said. "I'll get it painted."

"Another thing, I'm going up in the Hoodoos tomorrow and fetch that rotten little Cliff kid home. Call Pap and tell him I'll pick him up at seven Tuesday morning, just in case he's forgotten."

"Can I tell him not to bring a gun?"

"No. This time I want him to bring his twelve-gauge pump shotgun without the plugs and a box of double-ought buck shells. And a pistol of his choice."

"Holy cow!"

"This is all secret stuff, Daisy. It may turn out to be nothing. And I don't want to look too much the fool if it does. So don't blab anything to the deputies. Those who need to know will know."

"Gotcha, boss."

"One more thing, Daisy."

"What's that?"

"You're the best darn secretary I've ever had."

Tears welled up in Daisy's eyes.

"Thanks, boss."

People lead hard lives. If there was one thing Tully had learned in his ten years as sheriff, it was that.

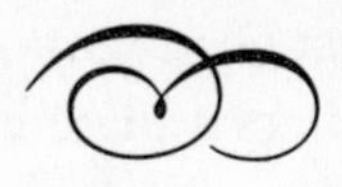

Chapter 43

On his way home that evening, he stopped by Jacob's Grocery and picked up a half pound of peppered bacon for the grouse. In the produce department he selected half a dozen salad ingredients. When he got home he salted the two grouse and put them in the oven to bake, with a couple slices of bacon pinned to each with a toothpick. You couldn't buy a meal like this in New York City for a thousand dollars a plate, he was willing to bet.

By four thirty he was getting tired. He had begun to think that inviting Susan out for dinner hadn't been such a great idea. But if not now, when? Perhaps never. He drove back into town and picked her up at her office.

"I am beat!" she said. "If you weren't such an entertaining gentleman, I'd call off this date right now."

"After a couple of martinis, I'm even more of an entertaining gentleman," Tully said. "The dinner I got cooking will revive you, guaranteed. Roast grouse on a bed of wild rice. Cost you a thousand dollars a plate in New York City."

"I have to admit it sounds wonderful. How about the martinis? And the foot massage?"

"Oh, they're ready, too."

Tully awoke at six o'clock Monday morning. He was fully dressed and lying on his couch. Two empty martini glasses sat on the coffee table, a plastic toothpick in each. The remains of the grouse dinner still sat on the table. Susan snored loudly in the big fat easy chair. She was covered to her chin with an afghan throw. She too was fully clothed, Tully saw, except possibly for her feet. Tully could remember the foot massage but not covering her with the afghan. He doubted he'd ever forget that foot massage.

He walked over and shook Susan. Her eyes popped open. She looked around, then up at Tully.

"Good Lord!" she said.

"Must have been a pretty wild date," Tully said. "Wish I could remember it."

"Me, too," she said.

She stretched and yawned. "You know something, Bo?"

"What's that?"

"This was the best sleep I've had in years. No offense."

"None taken. Uh-oh, I've got to go. I've got a Jeep Wrangler parked in the garage, Susan. The keys are on the nail by the sink. You can drive it to the office when you're ready. Heck, use it as long as you want. I'll be in touch, okay?"

"Okay. It seems so early. And you're up and dressed already."

"Oh, I never take my clothes off at night. Just have to put them back on again in the morning."

"Very efficient," she said.

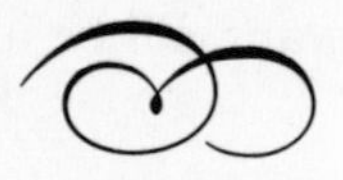

Chapter 44

When he got to the office, Jan Whittle was sitting in his chair staring out the window at Lake Blight. Daisy had been right, the view of the lake and mountains was spectacular. Maybe he wouldn't have the window painted after all. A shot from a boat bobbing around on the water would be awfully difficult.

"Can you think of anyone who would want to shoot me, Jan?" he said.

"No. Except maybe a grade-school principal who can't get you up in the mountains to look for Glen Cliff."

"It so happens that is exactly what I am doing today. I figured the snow would bring him down, but it hasn't."

"You better hope he isn't dead."

Tully laughed. "I was hoping just the opposite of that. Every year that kid runs off somewhere, the last two, somewhere up in the mountains. If I had my way, I'd leave him up there."

"Fortunately, you don't have your way."

Tully pulled a pair of insulated hunting boots and wool socks out of the closet. He sat down in a chair and began putting them on. Jan sat in his chair at his desk and watched him. He glanced nervously at her. "What?"

"Nothing. I was just remembering you when we were in grade school together."

"You remember sixth grade?" Tully said, lacing up one of the boots.

"Of course."

"Do you remember that you were my girlfriend that year?"

"I thought I might be, but we never even talked."

"Yeah," Tully said, "that's how it was done back then. Probably a pretty good idea for extending a relationship. How are you and old Darrel getting along, by the way?"

"Fine."

"Too bad."

"Do you remember that you gave me a present at Christmas when we were in sixth grade?"

"Yeah, I remember, but it was my mother's fault. I asked her what I should give a girl for a present, and she said, 'You can't go wrong with some nice soap.'"

"I see. Well, I guess a bar of Lifebuoy is pretty nice soap. I think it was the one back then that had the commercial claiming it got rid of B.O., body odor."

"Sorry about that. I always thought you were the best-smelling kid in class, not that that meant a whole lot in our sixth grade."

"You know what, Bo? I still have that bar of soap."

He glanced up. He could swear she had tears in her eyes. He seemed to be having that effect on women these days.

"Tell you what, Jan. Some night when Darrel plans to watch his favorite TV shows, maybe you and I could have dinner at Crabbs and talk over old times."

"The sheriff and the grade-school principal having dinner together at Crabbs? I think people would gossip shamefully. Thursday is his favorite TV night, though."

Tully smiled. "I'll give you a call."

"Okay, but please find the Cliff boy first."

Oh yeah, he thought. The Cliff boy.

Tully drove the Explorer up into the Hoodoo Mountains until he came to snow. Then he got out and chained up all four tires. He drove in two-wheel drive until the vehicle began to fishtail on the road. Then he shifted into four-wheel drive, and finally stopped when the Explorer started plowing snow with its radiator.

A dark cloud had risen over the Hoodoos and Tully could tell more snow was on the way. He hoped the Cliff boy would be where he expected him to be. He hauled his army-surplus snowshoes out of the SUV. Then he pulled his day pack out and put it on. A pair of bear-paw snowshoes were strapped to the pack. Carrying his other snowshoes, he waded up the road until the snow reached his knees. He strapped on the snowshoes and began the peculiar hip-swinging waddle he used with them. Two hours of this would make him think his crotch was on fire, but he hoped to find the kid before then. He reached the old mining camp sooner than he had expected and was relieved to see smoke coming from the chimney of one of the cabins. The trick now would be to keep the Cliff kid from shooting him. Or him from shooting the Cliff kid. When he got to the cabin, he took off the snowshoes and kicked open the door.

Glen Cliff was sitting on a bunk reading a book by light from a Coleman lantern. He stared at Tully, who was glancing about the room trying to locate the kid's rifle. It was leaning in a corner near the door.

"About time you showed up," Glen said.

Tully picked up the rifle, slipped the bolt out of it and put the bolt in his parka pocket. "I can tell you one thing, Glen, this is the last time I come up here looking for you. From now on, you die up here, that's fine with me."

"I was about ready to come down. The snow was getting too deep to move around much. I don't think even school is as boring as sitting in this cabin. I'll give school a try and see if it's as boring as I think."

"You better try it until you're out of high school."

Paperback books were scattered everywhere. One of them had a Blight County Library stamp on the back of it. Tully turned it over with the toe of his boot: *A Tale of Two Cities* by Charles Dickens. "You read all these?"

"Yeah. Some of them twice."

"Nothing like boredom, I guess, to make a young man further his education. You ever think about girls, Glen? In my day, they were the main reason I went to school."

"Girls are interesting, all right, but I wouldn't know the first thing about getting a girlfriend."

"All you have to do is pick out one and start talking to her. Maybe give her a gift."

"A gift? What kind of gift?"

"Soap is nice. You can't go wrong with soap."

"Soap!"

"Yeah, soap. You might want to avoid Lifebuoy, though."

Glen had spent the summer building up his cache of food and books in the old mine cabin. He and Tully left the books but loaded what was left of the tins of food into two cardboard boxes. They each carried a box as they left the cabin. Tully held his box on his shoulder with one hand and carried the rifle in his other hand. Glen carried the other box and an ax. It occurred to Tully that it might be a good idea to trade the boltless rifle for the ax, but Glen seemed satisfied to be leaving the mountains. The boy put on the bear paws and walked ahead, placing his smaller snowshoes in the tracks Tully had made coming in. While they were still on the crest of the ridge, he stopped and pointed off to the north.

"What's going on up there?"

"Where's there?" Tully said through his puffing and wheezing. He looked off in the direction the kid was pointing.

"Up there. It looks like the Last Hope Canyon. Every night I see vehicle lights coming around over the mountains and then disappearing down the canyon."

Tully stopped in mid-wheeze. "What kind of vehicles?"

"I don't know. It's a long way off. All I can see are the lights."

"What night was this?"

"Every night."

Tully dropped the boy off at the Cliff house. "Your father's not going to beat you or anything, is he?"

Glen laughed. "Not a chance. My mom may take a swipe at me, though. I think she worries."

"Somebody needs to, I suppose."

"Can I keep the bear paws?"

"I guess. Every kid needs a pair of snowshoes. By the way, before you go to school and tell Mrs. Whittle what a fine job I did rescuing you from a life-and-death situation, you might buy some Lifebuoy. And use it on yourself!"

Chapter 45

Pap was rocking in his chair on his porch and smoking one of his handmades. He got up a little stiffly, grabbed his pack with one hand, his pump shotgun with the other, and slowly made his way out to the Explorer. Tully got out and walked around to open the rear door for him.

"You're walking kind of funny this morning," Pap said.

"You should talk," Tully said. "I at least have an excuse. I went up in the mountains yesterday and got the Cliff kid. On snowshoes."

"Snowshoes?"

"Yeah."

"Snowshoes always make a man walk funny for a couple of days, like he's straddling a barrel."

"Yeah, a barrel with a fire inside it."

Tully stuffed the old man's gear in the back and shut the door. They both returned to the front of the vehicle and got in. Pap, as always, fussed with the seat belt. Tully leaned over and fastened it for him.

"You have Susan out for dinner?"

"Yeah. She spent the night."

Pap looked at him, then stared sadly out the windshield. "Oh to be seventy again," he said.

"Don't feel too sorry for yourself. Susan slept in my easy chair. I conked out on the couch."

"You think that makes me feel better," Pap said. Then he laughed. "I guess maybe it does."

They drove north toward Famine. The sun was out and there was a brisk wind, and the cottonwoods along the river were growing ever more bare, the last of the Cadmium Yellow Light leaves trailing out from them. Tully did not much care for cottonwoods. More than one person had been killed on a hot summer day by their huge dead limbs dropping soundlessly from high above. Then there were the sticky, bloody little buds that coated the feet of pets and their humans to be tracked into the carpets of houses. He did enjoy the smell of cottonwoods, in the fall, with their wet leaves on the ground.

Pap appeared to doze off as they roared through the morning sunshine. Tully was relieved when the old man roused himself and dug the makings of a cigarette out of his jacket pocket.

"So this thing is going down tonight?" he said.

"That's my plan, such as it is," said Tully. "I had Dave out doing some work."

"Dave the Indian?"

Tully laughed. "Yeah, Dave the Indian. He is a terrific tracker."

"He is that," Pap agreed.

"So if he found what I expected him to find, we go tonight, about midnight."

"Be careful you don't tell nobody about what you expected him to find," Pap grumbled.

"Don't worry. I won't."

As they approached the Littlefield ranch, Tully slowed down.

"We stopping here again?" Pap said. "I think you've got a thing for one of these ladies. Maybe both of them. If it's that Cindy Littlefield, though, it'll be a good lesson for old Vern."

"Cindy's pretty darn nice, all right, but it's the other one I got my eye on."

Tully pulled up in front of the Littlefield house, walked up to the door and rang the bell.

Cindy answered it. "Sheriff! Why, this is a surprise. Vern's still not back and I haven't heard from him."

"It's not Vern I'm here to see. It's your new cook."

"Dana? For heaven's sake, why?"

"I need to see her for a second."

Dana walked into the living room. She seemed surprised to see Tully at the door. "Sheriff Tully! What brings you back so soon?"

"I need to talk to you for just a moment."

Dana walked over and stood next to Cindy. "What is it?"

"Would you hold your wrists out like this?" Tully showed her how to hold her wrists.

"I guess so. You want me to hold them like this?"

"Perfect." Tully took a pair of handcuffs from the back of his belt and snapped them on her wrists.

Both Cindy and Dana stared down at the cuffs.

Dana blurted out a four-letter obscenity.

"What is this?" Cindy said. "Are you arresting her?"

"Yes, I am. Now, Cindy, if you would hold your wrists just exactly as Dana was so nice to do."

Cindy put both of her wrists behind her back.

"What are you arresting me for?"

"Harboring a fugitive from justice," Tully said.

"A fugitive from justice?"

Tully nodded at Dana. Cindy's mouth gaped open.

Dana asked how Tully had reached that conclusion, throwing in several very serious obscenities in the process.

"Your fingerprints on the Danielle Steel," he said. "We folks here in Blight County are generally pretty slow, but we do have a fairly sophisticated fingerprint-identification system."

Tully told Cindy the ride to jail would be a lot more comfortable if her hands were cuffed in front of her. She reluctantly held her wrists out and Tully snapped the cuffs on. He pulled both women through the door and took them out to the Explorer. He inserted them into the back seat and fastened a seat belt around each of them.

Pap had turned in his seat to study the prisoners.

"Howdy, ladies," he said. "My, this is quite a surprise. Bo seems to have developed a more direct approach with women than I ever did."

Both women told him what they thought of his observation.

"My, such language! You know, Bo," Pap said, "I can remember a time when even bad girls didn't talk that way. I think I preferred it."

"Me, too," said Tully. "But these may be bad-bad girls."

"Oh? In that case, I guess it might be all right."

"You all wait here a minute while I lock up the house," Tully said.

Once inside, he walked around until he found the den. As he expected, Vern Littlefield's gun case was there. All the slots were full. Tully squatted down so that he could read the calibers. The Remington .270 was there. It was possible, of course, that Vern had another .270 for elk, but Tully thought that extremely unlikely. And just as unlikely was any call from Vern on his cell phone, or any expectation that Vern would ever be coming home from his elk hunt. He looked around for Oscar the ferret, but the animal was apparently hiding. There being little chance the ferret had a criminal past, Tully took a carton of milk out of the refrigerator and poured some in a bowl. He put the bowl in the sink. He took a package of German sausages out of the refrigerator and dumped them into the sink alongside the bowl of milk. Next to the bowl of milk, he put a pan of water. He had no idea what pet ferrets ate, but figured he couldn't go too wrong with German sausages and milk. After taking care of Oscar, he walked into a bathroom that seemed to be part of Vern Littlefield's domain. There was a hairbrush on the counter containing several hairs. He spread a hand towel out on the counter and, using part of the towel to cover his hand, he picked up the brush and wrapped it in the towel, making a note to himself to obtain a warrant for search of the Littlefield residence for a hairbrush and a .270 rifle.

The little town of Famine seemed even quieter than usual as they drove down the main street. Tully parked alongside Ed's gas station.

"I have to run in here for a few minutes," Tully said to Pap. "Can you keep an eye on our prisoners and make sure they don't escape?"

"My pleasure," said Pap.

This was followed by an outburst of imaginative obscenities from the back seat.

"There's one I haven't heard in a while," Pap said. He took out the makings and started work on one of his hand-rolleds. This brought more obscenities from the back seat.

Tully walked into the station, plopped down in one of the chairs and put his feet up on another one. The girl at the counter smiled at him, and he smiled back. He picked up the day's copy of the *Lewiston Morning Tribune* and was perusing it when Ed came in from waiting on a customer.

"How's it going, Bo?"

"Pretty fair, considering." He didn't look up from the story he was reading. "Anything happening in Famine, Ed?"

"Not much. Things are pretty quiet. I see you and

Pap have a couple of nice looking women in your rig."

"Yup. If they'd lift up their wrists you could see the cuffs."

"No fooling! Why, the one is Cindy Littlefield! How come you're arresting them?"

"They've been bad."

"Bad! How bad?"

"At this moment, I don't rightly know that Cindy has been bad at all. But as I always say, hey, why take chances? Arrest everybody in sight and sort it all out later."

"You're starting to sound more like Pap every day."

"I expect so. I've been hanging out with him far too long."

The station bell rang. Tully looked up from his paper. Another red sheriff's Explorer had pulled in next to the gas pumps. Young Ernie Thorpe stepped out and came into the station.

"Howdy, Mr. Grange," he said. "Sheriff, you wanted me up here this morning?"

"You bet I did, Ernie. I got some prisoners for you to take back to the station."

"Those ladies sitting with Pap?"

"They're not exactly ladies, Ernie, as I'm sure you'll soon learn. And then there's Ed here."

"What!" said Ed. "You're kidding, right, Bo?"

"Afraid not, Ed. Put the cuffs on him, Ernie."

"I can't believe this! What's the charge?"

"I'll have to think about that, but I'm sure I can come up with something good. Don't worry about your station, Ed. I'll lock it up when I leave."

The deputy shoved Ed out through the door and put him in the front seat of the Explorer. He reached down and pulled up a chain fastened to a bolt in the floor. He snapped a lock on the end of the chain through Ed's cuffs. He then fastened Ed's seat belt.

Tully watched out the window. Then he glanced at the girl. She looked as if she was ready to faint. "Don't be upset," he said. "All this will work out fine. But I have a big favor to ask. Don't tell anybody what you just saw here, okay?" The girl nodded. "Good," he said. "Because if you talk at all about this, I would find out, and then you would be in big trouble."

"I won't say anything," she said.

"I'm sure you won't. Now put on your coat and go home."

The girl left. Deputy Thorpe got the two women out of Tully's SUV and put them in the back seat of his Explorer. Wisps of hair hung down Cindy's face. She looked as if she had been crying. Dana made an unfriendly gesture to him out the window with both hands. It's so hard to be popular, Tully thought. Ernie fastened Dana's seat belt and then walked around the car and fastened Cindy's. He locked all the car doors with his remote and walked back into the gas station.

"Nice work," Tully said.

"Thanks. I guess you want me back up here this evening."

"That's right. We might have some pretty heavy lifting around midnight. Keep it to yourself, though. Eliot will fill you in."

"Sounds interesting."

"I'm sure it will be. But don't expect any overtime pay."

"I haven't seen any yet."

Tully laughed. "Good boy!"

Ernie started back to his vehicle.

"You be careful with our prisoners," Tully said. "They could be a whole lot worse than I think they are."

"Yes, sir."

Tully watched Ernie's Explorer pull out and head back toward Blight City. He waved at the occupants. They didn't wave back. Then he walked around inside the station opening cupboards and drawers. Nothing of interest caught his attention. He went through the side door into the attached garage. He looked at the steel-topped workbench along one wall. Underneath were grimy drawers for tools and supplies. Tully opened them one by one and found only tools and supplies. The last two large bottom drawers had padlocks on them. Tully looked around the garage until he found a bolt cutter. He walked back and snipped off the lock of the first one. The drawer was packed with hundred-dollar bills. "Bingo!" he said. He picked one up and sniffed it. Then he put it back and snipped the lock off the other drawer. It contained small packages of marijuana. He went out to his car and returned with his camera. He shot several photos of the open drawers and then several photos of the workbench with the drawers still open. In the front office, he found a rack with new locks sealed in plastic on cardboard. He took two of them off the rack, tore them open and dropped the keys in his pocket. He walked back to the garage, closed the drawers and put a lock on each one. He rolled down the large doors of the garage and locked them. Then he put the Closed sign on the station's front door, and locked the door as he went out. Opening the rear of the Explorer, he dropped the bolt cutter into the cargo area. It simply was not a good idea to leave bolt cutters anywhere near padlocked drawers.

When he got back to the Explorer, Pap was asleep in the front seat, his head leaning against the window.

Chapter 46

Pap jerked awake when Tully opened the car door. He managed to fight off a yawn. "I see you sent Ed off in cuffs. Any particular reason?"

"There is now. I found a big drawer full of hundred-dollar bills."

"Does this mean we're rich?"

"No!"

"I was afraid you'd say that. I hate to break the news to you, Bo, but it ain't against the law to have a drawer full of bills. Stupid, yes, but not illegal."

"Next to that drawer I found a drawer filled with packages of marijuana, retail-size packages, like you'd sell to individuals for their own use."

"Sounds as if Ed had the corner on Famine dope sales," Pap said.

"That would be a reasonable assumption. I think he's also involved in a much larger scheme."

"What got you zeroing in on Ed?"

"Buck did. We were in the station when I told you we were going to head back to Blight City. Ed was standing right there, the only person in the station with us at the time, as you pointed out. I decided to stop at the Littlefields'. Buck must have passed us. The sniper on the hill had to think Buck was us. And somebody had to tip him off, so he could get in position."

"Or it could have been Ed himself."

"It could have been, but I don't think so. There's another thing, too."

"What's that?"

"The Jeep Grand Cherokee itself."

"You've got Ed and the Jeep tied together?"

"I think so. And then there's the overall operation. It came to me while I was getting a haircut."

"Maybe you should get a haircut more often. And here people think you're not smart enough to solve these murders."

Tully looked over at the old man. "But they know I've got you along."

"Why, there you go!"

Tully dug out his cell phone and called Daisy.

"What's up, Bo?"

"First, I want you to call Ed Grange's wife up in Famine and inform her that her husband has been arrested. Tell her the station is under police surveillance. Tell her that her phone is tapped and that if she calls anyone or leaves the house she will be arrested."

"Is that legal?"

"I don't know. Why do you ask?"

"No reason. Anything else?"

"Yes, but I can't think of it right now. Don't leave the office, don't go out for lunch. I need you right there. Order in a sandwich or something."

Tully could tell from the sound of her voice that she was pleased.

"You got it, boss. Where are you now?"

"We're right outside Ed's Gas-N-Grub in Famine. But we're heading out to Dave's House of Fry."

"Are you going to arrest Dave, too?"

"No, not yet, anyway. One way or another, this whole thing is going to be a done deal sometime tonight, if we can manage to keep the lid on it a little while longer."

He hung up.

Pap scratched the white stubble on his chin. "You know, Bo, the word is out by now, about the arrests and all. There's some real bad folks out there who have got themselves busy as bees. They could be packing up to beat it out of the county even as we speak. And we don't have a clue who they are. You might be able to squeeze some names out of Ed, but I imagine he's a whole lot more scared of the bad guys than he is of us."

"Ed is one of the bad guys. I figure he's the one who set up the ambush."

"You mean the guy in the right back seat?"

"That's the one. I had Lurch run a little test on the Jeep Grand Cherokee."

"A test?"

"Yeah. Those fellows rented the Jeep at the Spokane Airport at ten P.M. They drove down to Blight. It takes nearly a whole tank of gas to get here from Spokane. There's no gas station open that late at night between here and Spokane. We know the ambush took place exactly at three thirty-eight in the morning, because the one guy had his wristwatch clipped by a bullet. The Jeep rolled forward in drive and hit the berm across the Last Hope Road. So the engine continued to run from three thirty-eight in the morning until a little before we found it. Remember, the engine was still hot?"

"That's right, it was. You hooted like a scalded owl."

"So they had to get the gas tank filled up somewhere."

"Ed filled the tank?"

"There's no other place. No other person."

"But what makes you think Ed set up the ambush?"

"He had to be waiting for them at the station. So my guess is he's the one that led them out to the Last Hope Road. Who else?"

"I think you may be right. But I'm not at all sure all this stuff you're doing is legal."

"Hey, it's the Blight way. Isn't that what you used to say, Pap?"

The old man shook his head. "I appreciate you saying that, Bo. Just don't get yourself killed tonight. More important, don't get me killed."

Bo laughed. He put the Explorer in drive and pulled out onto the main street of Famine. The town was quiet. Too quiet, he wanted to say, but wasn't up to Pap's ridicule.

They pulled into the House of Fry parking lot. It was nearly empty. Dave was standing on the front porch.

"Paying customers, I hope," he said as they walked up.

"Always," Tully said.

"I could use some lunch," Pap said.

"Yeah, maybe we'll eat something," Tully said. "We're not likely to get much chance later."

"I don't know what you've been doing," Dave said, "but you're ruining my business."

"I arrested Ed Grange," Tully told him. "Along with Cindy Littlefield and the new so-called cook, Dana Cassidy."

"I can't believe it. Cindy! What charge?"

"Dana has an outstanding warrant for dealing drugs. Got Cindy for harboring a fugitive."

Dave shook his head. "You're liable to have all of Famine in jail."

"I'm beginning to think so."

"C'mon in," Dave said. "I'll have the cooks fix you some lunch. It's not as though they're overworked right now."

Tully selected a table in back, where they could talk without being overheard.

Carol came over and took their orders. Tully and Pap each ordered the World Famous House of Fry Burger along with the Endless Fries and coffee.

"If I don't get done with this case soon," Tully said, "the cholesterol alone will kill me. So where's Deedee?"

"Gone," said Dave. "Along with most of my customers. Deedee moved to Blight City. I guess the pay is better down there, and they don't pinch as hard. Don't know what happened to my customers. Maybe they're afraid somebody will show up and spray the place with machine guns. I'm beginning to think that could be a distinct possibility."

Pap looked around the café. "Maybe you should lock the front door."

"Yeah, that would help business a lot."

"I meant just while Bo and I are here."

Dave gave him an exasperated look. "Anyway, Bo, I got the info you wanted."

Pap looked at Tully. "What info is that?"

"I sent Dave up to the Last Hope Mine to put his tracking skills to use."

"Like you told me," Dave said, "I went up in the morning, about nine o'clock. Hiked up from the berm. There were the tracks you made when you went up there with Susan, both going up and coming back down. You were right about the other tracks. The ones coming down don't match the ones going up."

"Good. I had Lurch make casts of them."

"There wasn't a soul around, either at the dam or the mine."

Carol brought a coffeepot, poured them each a cupful, then left. She made the rounds of the few other diners, refilling their cups. The three men at the table watched her, as if Carol were on an important mission.

"The mine entrance was blasted shut thirty, forty years ago," Pap said. "So what's your interest in it?"

"Think about it," said Tully. "Suppose they started using the mine again."

Pap shook his head. "The Last Hope ran out of gold

decades ago. That's why they blew the entrance, keep kids and people from fooling around in there."

"What if they made a new entrance?" Tully said.

"That's exactly what they did," Dave put in. "Sometime in the last few years. It was a devil of a thing to find, too, not much bigger than a rabbit hole. I found a bunch of fresh rock dumped down over the edge of the road, and then I was pretty sure it had come from a new tunnel. Took me almost all day, but I found it. The entrance was covered with a slab of shale, or at least something that looks like shale. I didn't go in, of course, but judging from its location the new tunnel is about twenty feet long and cuts into the mine behind the old entrance. Nobody would even notice it, unless that was what they were looking for."

"I see where you're going with this," Pap said.

"I should hope so," Tully said. "A mine makes a perfect year-round growing environment. The U.S. Forest Service has been growing tree seedlings up in a Kellogg mine for years. The mine has water and warmth. All they have to do is pipe in daylight. So our bad guys set up grow lights, run power to them from the dam, and nobody notices a sudden surge in the use of electricity."

"Right," Dave said, "and an abnormal increase in the use of electricity is one of the giveaways, if, say, you're growing large crops of marijuana with grow lights. That's the main reason I haven't done it."

"But Littlefield has his own electricity," Pap said. "His dam is in the same canyon as the Last Hope."

"Just to be sure," Tully said, "I checked on Littlefield's sales of electricity to Central Electric. Four years ago it dropped to half the usual amount, with a normal rainfall and a normal snow pack in the Hoodoo Mountains during all those years. So what happened four years ago? Vern started himself a huge underground greenhouse in a mine."

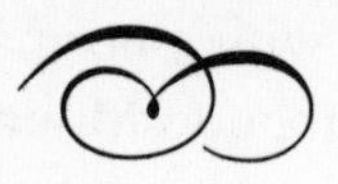

Chapter 47

Back in the Explorer, Pap rolled himself another cigarette and lit it. "You know, Bo," he said, "I'm not too fond of the idea of crawling through that twenty-foot tunnel into the mine. They could have some guy guarding it, just waiting to blast us."

"So what other options do we have?"

"Let's see now. Well, we could chuck a stick of dynamite into the little tunnel and seal 'em all up inside."

"Then what?"

"What do you mean, then what? We seal them up inside."

"And leave them?"

"Of course. Think of all the money it would save, the trials, prison time, feeding and entertaining them and like that. Of course prison time is assuming you get a conviction in the first place. Hey, it's the Blight way."

"Yeah, it would be that, all right. But forget it. We're going in. You don't have to if you don't want to."

"Ah, Bo, I was just pulling your leg. Of course I'm going in. I don't have anything else to do. Except maybe live."

"Good. I need at least one person along I know isn't bothered by shooting other human beings."

"Thanks. I appreciate you saying that."

They drove back through Famine. Half a dozen people were gathered in front of the General Store. They were in serious, animated conversation. When the sheriff's red Explorer approached, they stopped talking and stared.

Tully lowered his side window. "Howdy," he said. "How you all doing?"

No one responded.

Tully ran his window back up.

"You don't seem too popular around here," Pap said.

"Don't seem to be."

"Where are we headed?"

"Out to the old Littlefield hotel."

"I'm sorry I asked. That place is a bit too spooky for me."

"There weren't any spooks. The guy I saw out in the hallway made a tremendous racket getting away. I assume ghosts don't make any racket when they run down a flight of stairs."

"You should have shot him."

"I was reaching for my gun when he got away."

"You said you couldn't recognize him, right?"

"Right. It was too dark. But there was something about him that seemed kind of familiar. I've been thinking a lot about that, and I've got a feeling it was Lem Scragg. He was long and skinny like that."

Pap ground out the butt of his cigarette in the ashtray. "He obviously didn't know we were sacked out in there."

"I don't think he did. That's why I had the vehicles put in that shed. But he was up there for some reason."

"If it was Lem, that means he probably was tied in with Littlefield some way."

"Yeah," Tully said. "And that's odd, because the Littlefields and the Scraggs have been enemies practically forever. But I don't know for sure it was Lem. I'll ask him, if we run into him tonight."

"You think the Scragg brothers were the shooters on the Last Hope Road, don't you?"

"Don't you?"

"Yeah. I just didn't want to say so."

Tully's cell phone buzzed. It was Susan. "Is this a bad time, Bo?"

"No. Any time you call is a good time. Pap and I are driving down the highway right at the moment."

"I don't mean to bother you," she said. "First, though, I'd like to apologize for flaking out on you after the delicious dinner the other night."

"It was probably the foot massage."

"Foot massage?" she said.

"Never mind. Pap's getting all excited here."

"That'll be the day," Pap mumbled, "that I get excited over feet."

"I really had a wonderful time," Susan said. "I'm just sorry I flaked out. I was totally exhausted."

Tully had been so tired he could scarcely remember much about the evening himself.

"I completely understand," he said.

"Now I have a favor to ask."

"Shoot."

"Could I stay at your place tonight? I know you'll be gone all night. I just can't stand to stay at the B and B any longer, and my apartment won't be ready until tomorrow."

"You want to move into my place?"

He could practically see Pap's ears prick up.

"No, I mean only for tonight," Susan said, obviously embarrassed.

"I just said that for Pap's benefit," Tully told her. "He gets so few thrills anymore I couldn't resist. Sure, it's okay. Stay as long as you like. My bedroom is the one on the left. Don't even look in there. The guest room is the one on the right."

"Thank you. By the way, I was looking at those watercolors on the courthouse walls again. They're very good. I had no idea you were such a good painter."

"Thanks. Many of the Blight folks who see the paintings still don't think I'm a painter at all."

"Well, I am impressed."

"There's one," said Tully. "By the way, I guess you made it into town all right with the Wrangler."

"Yes, and I loved it. I'll drive it back tonight with my stuff, if that's okay. I can leave my car in the city garage."

Pap heaved a long sigh as he stared at some cows out the window.

"I've got to go," Tully said. "Pap is heaving sighs."

"Yes, I know you're busy. I just wanted to thank you, Bo. Take care."

"You bet."

Tully punched the Off button on the cell phone. Pap said, "That's a fine thing. You barely know the woman and already you got her moving in with you. I've made that mistake a few times myself. Means nothing but trouble. Fun, though."

"That's you, of course. This situation is totally proper. She's moving into the guest room for one night. I was trying to remember if I left anything on the floor in my bedroom, like pants and underwear and dirty plates, in case she can't resist looking in there."

"I remember once a lady I was staying with got up early to go to work," Pap said. "I peeked out from under the covers, pretending I was still asleep. My pants were out in the middle of the floor, and when she walked by she kicked them clear over against the wall!"

"There's nothing lower than kicking a man's pants," Tully said.

"That's the way I felt about it. I got up and left and never spoke to her again."

"That probably taught her a good lesson."

Tully turned into the long driveway that led up to the Littlefield house. He took the 9 mm Glock pistol out of the holster and laid it on the seat. Pap pulled the shotgun out of its clip on the dashboard.

"I like a shotgun," he said.

"Slugs, ought bucks, alternated," Tully said.

"Serious stuff. You go in the brush after wounded grizzlies with this?"

"Could," Tully said. "Haven't yet, though."

He pulled up in front of the house. No one stirred from inside it or from any of the other buildings. He drove the mile down the rutted road to the hotel and stopped. No sign of anyone there.

"By the way," Pap said, "what are we looking for?"

"Don't know. But whoever I saw that night was here for some reason."

"What makes you think the guy was tied into the killings on the Last Hope Road?"

"Would you stop asking questions!"

"Just curious," Pap said.

They got out of the Explorer and went through the front door of the hotel. Tully carried the Glock down at his side and Pap rested the shotgun on his shoulder, the safety off and his finger resting on the side of the trigger guard.

"Try not to shoot anyone," Tully whispered.

The old man snorted.

"I don't think what we're looking for will be on the ground floor," Tully said. "So let's start with the second floor."

The stairs groaned and creaked with every step they took.

"I don't think we're going to surprise anyone," Pap said, no longer bothering to whisper.

"I guess not," Tully said. "I don't recall the stairs making so much noise last time."

"Maybe that's because we didn't expect somebody to jump out and shoot us."

When they reached the second floor, Tully pointed

down the hallway. "Pap, you work your way down there. Check every room. I'll take the other way."

"You got it, Sheriff."

Tully watched Pap do the first few doors of his hallway. The old man would turn the doorknob, raise the shotgun to firing position and push open the door with the barrel.

Looks like he's done this before, Tully thought, moving off down the other hallway. All the rooms he tried were empty of everything but dust. Then he reached the last room. He tried the doorknob. It was locked. Pap was already moving down the hallway toward him. He motioned for him to hurry up. Pap continued at the same pace.

"What's the hurry?" he said.

"This door is locked," Tully told him.

"So?"

"Can you pick a lock?"

"I'll give it a try."

"Be my guest," Tully said, stepping to one side.

Pap blew the lock away with the shotgun. He pushed the door open with the barrel.

Tully reacted to the shot with a ten-letter obscenity.

"I didn't know you knew that one," Pap said.

"You're a crazy old man!" Tully said.

"Listen, who's going to care? This thing is going down tonight."

Three bales of marijuana were stacked against one wall of the room. The bales were sealed with plastic sheets. Assorted tools, some scuba diving valves and regulators were piled in a cardboard box. Several air tanks were scattered about the floor. Wet suits hung along one wall. A table had been made out of a sheet of plywood and two sawhorses. Along with assorted scuba gear, a scoped .223 Ranch Rifle and a pearl-handled .45 automatic lay on the table.

"Well, there you go," said Tully.

"Holt's forty-five you think?"

"Don't know for sure, but I'd bet on it."

"Look at all the scuba gear," Pap said. "Why would someone stash scuba gear up here?"

"I can't imagine Lem Scragg as a scuba diver. Lake Blight is the only place to scuba dive around here. And there is nothing to find in Lake Blight."

"Certainly not fish," Pap said.

"I suppose we could leave," Tully said, "and no one would know we had discovered this cache of grass, except some fool blew away the lock."

"If some fool hadn't blown away the lock, we wouldn't have found the marijuana and the guns."

"I suppose," Tully said. "One thing it does make pretty clear is that Littlefield is involved in this. Except he's probably already dead."

"You don't think he's hiding out?"

"Nope. I think the night of the killing he drove in over the mountains and parked up by the Last Hope Mine. He wanted to see how the ambush went down but didn't want anybody to know he had been there. He walked down the road from the mine and hid back in the woods. Holt killed him by chance."

"So what did the ambushers do with the body?"

"Don't know. If the Scragg boys were involved, they

would have dropped it down a prospect hole back in the mountains. After the ambushers found the body, they probably figured out that Littlefield had parked his vehicle up at the mine. They sent someone up the road to drive the vehicle to Vern's hunting camp. That way his disappearance could always be explained away by saying he got lost while hunting in the mountains. Anyway, that explains the different tracks. Littlefield's were those going down and those going up belonged to whoever drove the truck away. Lurch took casts of both sets of tracks, so we shouldn't have too much trouble matching them up with the feet they belong to."

"You seem to have this whole thing figured out," Pap said.

"I've spent a lot of time thinking about it. But my feeling is there's probably not a single adult person in all of Famine who doesn't know more about this mess than we do."

"Might have to arrest the whole town."

"Don't think I'm not considering it," Tully said.

"It's what I'd recommend," Pap said. "Probably be doing everybody in Famine a favor. You'd be a hero."

When they got back to the Explorer, Tully called the office on his cell phone.

Daisy answered. "Sheriff's office. How may I help you?"

Tully thought the greeting had a bit of class. He had come up with it himself.

"Hi, Daisy. Put Eliot on, will you?"

"You bet."

She covered the mouthpiece with her hand, but he

still heard her yell, "Hey, Herb! Bo wants you on Line Two!"

Maybe, he thought, there's still some work to do. Herb came on. "What's up, Bo?"

"How are our two lady captives doing in jail?"

"Cindy Littlefield has been crying her eyes out. Probably her first time in the slammer. The other one, Dana, is tough as nails. I kind of doubt Mrs. Littlefield knows anything, and Dana simply isn't going to talk, at least until you get that mess cleaned up."

"What I need from you, Herb, is a couple of deputies up here at the Littlefield ranch. They're to arrest anyone that shows up. There's an old hotel building about a mile down a rutted road west of the ranch house. Put two men in that hotel. Tell them I don't want them upstairs at all but to stay on the main floor. Seal off the second floor. Anyone comes into the hotel, I don't care who, put the cuffs on them and keep them there."

"Anything else?"

"Yes. Get Lurch up to the hotel. Tell him to photograph everything in Room 28, check everything in it for prints, then pack it all up and bring it into the station."

"Don't we need a warrant?"

"A what?"

"Never mind."

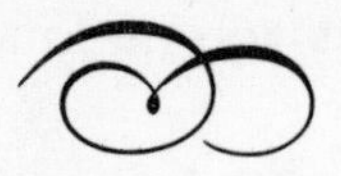

Chapter 48

Dave closed the House of Fry early that night and sent all the help home. Tully held a meeting there with Dave, Pap, Herb and the three deputies. They sat around a table in back drinking coffee.

"Okay," Tully said, "here's the plan. First thing I've got to tell you is that we may be outgunned and outmanned. The bad guys may have automatic weapons. We'll have pistols and shotguns. So nobody has to go who doesn't want to. Except me. Any questions so far?"

"What happens to us if we drop out?" Brian Pugh asked.

"Nothing," Tully said. "Except I throw you down a flight of stairs and break all your bones."

"Count me in then," said Pugh. Everyone laughed.

Tully explained that the place they were going into was the old Last Hope Mine, the entrance to which had been dynamited shut forty years before.

"The Last Hope Road is where those three guys were shot, right?" said Ernie Thorpe.

"That's right, three, counting the guy hanging over the Scragg fence. There was probably a fourth victim, too. We could find out about the fourth guy tonight, if we're lucky."

Chet Mason said, "I've got a question."

Tully nodded at him.

"Whoever's in the mine, do you think they're expecting us?"

"By now I'm pretty sure they know something is going down soon, but they probably don't think it's tonight. Now here's the plan. There's a new entrance. It's a very narrow tunnel but only about twenty feet long. Dave will go in first, because he's a tracker and an Indian."

"Wait a minute!" Dave said. "I'm a tracker, all right, but I was lying about being an Indian."

"In that case, I'll go in first," Tully said.

He explained that if there was a guard at the new tunnel's entrance, the raid was pretty much over. The first guy in might get killed, but the others should have all the bad guys trapped inside.

"As far as we can tell, there is only the one entrance and exit. You shouldn't have to wait too long for them to come out and surrender."

"Why don't we just wait for them to come out and surrender?" Ernie Thorpe asked. "Catch them on the way home?"

"Because," said Tully, "there is always the chance that

somewhere there is another exit we don't know about. The idea is we surprise them and catch them with the goods."

Chet Mason said, "Let me see if I've got this straight, Bo. You drop down into the main mine tunnel. Aren't they going to see you?"

"They would if that was the main workplace," Tully said. "But the main workplace should be several hundred yards inside the mine, where it's warm. Water wouldn't be a problem for them, because, at least in the mines I've been in, water is running all over the place. So they hauled in dirt, piped in some daylight from Littlefield's dam and generator and they were in the big time marijuana-growing business. The operation is so good, in fact, that some mob guys from L.A. decided they wanted in on it. Those guys are in the Blight City morgue right now. So you can expect that the folks we're going up against are pretty tough customers."

Tully asked if there were any more questions. The deputies looked at each other and shrugged.

"How about you, Pap?"

"There's a good chance there will be blood spilled tonight," Pap said. "Maybe quite a lot of it, maybe some of it ours. You got that contingency taken care of?"

"Yeah, I do," Tully said. "We go in at midnight sharp. Every ambulance in Blight City will be within ten minutes of the mine by then."

"How about the berm across the road?"

"I've got that taken care of, too. We'll also have

some backup from the State Police. They just won't be going into the mine, at least not at first."

Tully looked at his watch. "It's nine thirty. We have a couple of hours before we take off for the mine. You got time to grab a little shuteye, sit back and relax, play cards, whatever."

The deputies laughed.

"You're a funny guy, Bo," Brian Pugh said.

Tully shrugged.

Dave said, "Tell you what. Who wants one of Dave's World Famous House of Fry Burgers?"

He got a unanimous round of applause.

Tully sat down next to Pap.

"Almost like the old days," Tully said. "The only thing missing is no Deedee to fuss over you."

"Win some, lose some," Pap said. "Actually, Deedee was a bit young for me."

"You're right about that. I doubt she was out of her twenties. More my speed."

"What's your speed, Bo?"

"Anything legal."

"I guess that Susan is legal. She apparently shows some interest in you."

"A little bit. Of course I haven't had an opportunity to turn on the full force of my charm."

"Probably a good thing," Pap said. "Sooner or later that seems to wipe out your romances."

"I don't think it's so much my charm. It's more a matter of my pants in the middle of the floor."

"Yeah, that's a bad one."

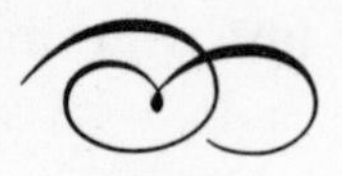

Chapter 49

Pap, Herb Eliot and Ernie Thorpe rode with Tully. Brian Pugh and Chet Mason rode with Dave in his pickup truck. Approaching the gate on the Last Hope Mine Road, Tully drove slowly ahead of the pickup, his spotlight playing back and forth through the trees ahead and on both sides. No signs of gunmen lurking there. Tully stopped in front of the berm. He got out of the Explorer. Lights came on to his right in the woods. A large truck was parked there. A D8 Caterpillar tractor was alongside it. The headlights of the tractor illuminated the berm. Tully walked over to the tractor. Amos Kauffman was sitting on the Cat.

"You ready, boy?" Amos said.

"I'm ready, Amos. Take out the berm, then back off and let us go through with the vehicles. Then drive the Cat up to the dam and knock down the gate across the road that leads down to the water."

Amos nodded and started the Cat. A great plume of

smoke rose in the air. The yellow beast growled forward and wiped out the berm in one pass, then backed off to the side. Tully gave Amos a thumbs-up and then drove up the road followed by Dave's pickup.

They passed the gated entrance to the dam. Down below, the dark water of the reservoir stretched far up the narrow canyon. They went by the old entrance to the mine. Pap had the shotgun pointed out his open window. They came to a parking area. Among the vehicles parked there were a dozen ATVs and Lucas's old school bus. Tully pulled into the parking area and stopped. Dave's pickup turned in next to them. Dave, Brian and Chet got out.

"Doesn't seem to be any lookout up here," Dave whispered.

"I sure didn't see or hear anything," Tully said. "If there was one, maybe he slipped away into the woods."

"Maybe," Dave said. "I think, though, that they're just not expecting us."

Pap said, "Lend me those bolt cutters, Bo."

"They're in the back of the Explorer."

The old man got out the bolt cutter, walked around and snipped one of the leads to the battery on each of the ATVs. The others stood in the darkness watching him, listening to the snip-snip of the bolt cutter.

"Not a bad idea," said Dave. "That way if any of them gets past us, he's going to be on foot."

"There's that," Tully said. "And then there's the fact that the old man loves bolt cutters. I guess how this gang gets in here is they ride in over the mountain from Littlefield's ranch."

"Has to be that way," Dave said.

Pap returned from his snipping and put the bolt cutter in the back of the Explorer. He was smiling.

Ernie Thorpe came over.

"It's almost midnight," he said.

"Yeah," said Dave. "The new entrance is just over on the other side of these ATVs. Let's go."

Tully didn't like the idea of being the point man through the narrow tunnel, but he couldn't very well send anyone else. There had been no volunteers. Pap would have been delighted to go first, of course, but Tully knew he would never hear the end of it if he let him.

"Herb, you stay outside and guard the entrance. We don't want to get trapped in there."

"My pleasure, boss."

Dave and Tully lifted the piece of shale away from the opening of the new tunnel. It was surprisingly light. Tully suspected it wasn't rock at all, but made of some kind of artificial substance that could be easily moved. He peeked over the edge. Below him was a shallow pit that had been blasted out of the rock. The tunnel extended at a downward slant from the pit to the old mine. He lowered himself into the pit and peered into the tunnel. It was dark from one end to the other. As his eyes grew accustomed to the dark, he could make out a faint glow of light at the far end.

He took a deep breath and started crawling through the tunnel on his hands and knees, the 9 mm Glock tucked back in its holster. Someone had laid several thicknesses of old carpet along the floor of the tunnel, which made the crawling a good deal less painful. The tunnel opened onto the floor of the mine. He peeked around the edge of the opening. Far off down the mine he could see a light and hear the murmur of voices. He could make out rusted rails for ore cars still in place on the floor of the mine. As he and Dave had suspected, the old timbers were now accompanied by new timbers as far as he could see. Tully now knew the reason for the brief logging operation on Littlefield land.

He slid out into the mine. He directed his flashlight back into the tunnel and blinked it once. He soon heard the scuffling sounds of crawling.

Dave was first out. The others emerged one by one, Pap bringing up the rear.

"Just like old times," Pap whispered.

Tully knew there was a big smile on his face, even though he couldn't see it.

"No killing unless absolutely necessary," he whispered back.

Ernie Thorpe whispered, "Man, this is spooky."

Chet Mason whispered, "I can smell the marijuana from here. You could get high just breathing the air."

"I don't want any of you high," Tully said. "Everybody walk quietly. The closer we get to the light, the better we'll be able to see. With any luck, we'll take them all by surprise, and there won't be any shooting."

They moved off down the mine, three in front and three behind. The murmur of the voices ahead grew louder. There was an occasional laugh. Soon they could make out words. Two men were talking about fishing.

Tully heard the words ". . . maggots mostly." The warmth and humidity increased steadily. Water drizzled down from overhead.

As they neared the light, they could make out a long line of tables containing hundreds of green plastic garden pots. The pots were empty. Beyond the empty pots, a heavy clear plastic curtain had been drawn between the rock walls. Shadowy figures could be seen moving about behind the curtain.

Tully and his deputies moved slowly along the tables, bent over as low as they could stand it. From time to time, Tully heard a moan from them. He felt like moaning himself. When at last he reached the plastic curtain, he stuck his Glock into a gap at one side and flung it open. He stepped into the light.

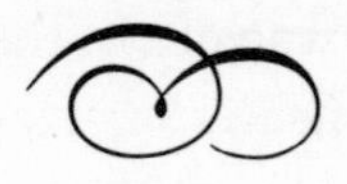

Chapter 50

A couple dozen men and women, residents of Famine, turned and stared at him. Tully in fact had seen some of them before, gray, flabby men and women, on the streets and in the stores and certainly at Ed's gas station, getting five gallons of gas in their tanks and their windows washed. Some of them wore bib overalls. Most were dressed in jeans. All of them wore T-shirts splotched with sweat. Tully recognized one man because of his earflap cap. He seemed to be supervising the work. Large pots of marijuana, some with plants reaching nearly to the rock ceiling, covered the tables stretching off into the distance. Some of the workers were cutting down plants, others were placing them in a contraption that compressed the stalks and leaves into tight bales and then wrapped them in heavy plastic sheets.

Lister Scragg leaned against a rock wall, a shotgun hanging by a sling from his shoulder. A cigarette dangled from the bottom lip of his gaping mouth. Old

Lucas, wearing his earflap cap even in the warmth of the mine, stood across from him, holding a rifle.

"Police!" Tully shouted. "Get your hands up!"

The workers continued to stare at Tully. No hands went up.

Pap, Dave and the deputies stormed in. Lister dropped behind a table, the weapon coming off his shoulder. An instant later, several plants flew apart and the rocks above Tully's head exploded as Lister fired from below the table. Workers dropped to the floor screaming and swearing as they crawled under the tables. Pap fired his shotgun into the rocks behind Lister's head. The rocks sprayed like shrapnel under the table. Lister staggered up and backwards, holding the bloody side of his head with one hand. He no longer held the weapon.

"Don't shoot!" he screeched. "Don't shoot! I been hit."

Pap had his finger on the trigger.

"Stop!" cried Tully.

Pap moved his finger reluctantly off the trigger.

Tully was sweeping his Glock back and forth, watching for anyone who came up with a weapon.

"This is the Sheriff of Blight County," Tully yelled. "Everybody in here is under arrest! Come out from under the tables with your hands up! Anyone holding a weapon will be shot!"

Bit by bit the workers, dazed and sullen, emerged from under the tables. Some of the women cried. They looked like housewives and farm workers, their hair wrapped in bandanas or covered with old felt hats or fits-all caps. Most of the men seemed older, their bellies swelling out their overalls, their jaws covered with gray stubble. Several had the brown juice of chewing tobacco dribbling down their chins. No one in the crowd appeared to be a prosperous drug dealer.

Brian Pugh moved behind one of the tables, his shotgun at the ready. Holding the gun in one hand, he grabbed Lister by the arm and jerked him back to where Tully was standing. Dave slid behind the table and picked up the shotgun.

Except for the forest of marijuana plants undergoing harvest, Tully felt as if he had interrupted a Famine bingo party.

The room fell into a dazed silence, with only the sound of water dripping and dribbling from the rock ceiling. Then, off in the distant darkness of the tunnel, Tully heard someone running deeper into the mine. A lot of good that will do him, he thought.

Then Lister blurted out, "Wasn't me shot those guys down on the road. It was them. I'm not taking the fall for them."

"Who's them?"

"Them!" He pointed off down the mine with a bloody hand.

What had bothered Tully since they had entered the mine suddenly came to him. The bales of marijuana both here and at the hotel were too big to go through the narrow entrance tunnel!

"Quick, Lister, and you'd better not lie or I'll turn you over to Pap."

Pap grinned his evil grin at Lister.

"What?" cried Lister.

"Is there another exit from the mine?"

"Sure. Down there a couple hundred yards or so. Comes out down on the dam's reservoir."

"Brian, Chet, Ernie!" Tully yelled. "You three search these characters here. If you find a weapon on someone, cuff him. Those with IDs, get the names and addresses and put them on the bus and take them home. Those without IDs go to jail. And cuff the guy with the earflap cap. I want him taken in. Take those rubber boots off of him, too, and sack them up as evidence."

"You got it, boss," Chet said. "How about this character?" He indicated Lister.

"Cuff him and take him to my vehicle. Have the medics wipe some of the blood off of him. Makes us look bad."

The faint sounds of sirens drifted into the mine.

"I ain't going down for this," Lister said.

"We'll talk, Lister," Tully told him, "but not right now."

Pap and Dave were already in the small entrance tunnel. Tully scrambled through after them.

As expected, the ATVs and the old school bus were still there. "You need help?" Herb yelled at them.

"No, we got it covered," Tully shouted back at him. "Keep guarding the entrance."

He grabbed a rifle and handed it to Pap, who threw his shotgun on the ground. Tully grabbed a portable spotlight and a portable bullhorn out of the Explorer.

The three of them ran down over the bank toward the reservoir. When they came to where the rock walls dropped sharply down into the canyon, they stopped and sat down. The water was low, far down on the dam.

Pap was wheezing. "Okay if I build myself a smoke?"

"Go ahead," Tully said. "If you can build it and still hold a rifle."

"Sure. I could roll a cigarette paper with my toes if I had to."

It seemed colder close to the reservoir, particularly after the warmth of the mine. Tully turned up the collar on his jacket.

"Just exactly what are we supposed to be looking for?" Dave said.

"If I'm not mistaken," Tully said, "any minute now three or four men are going to come paddling a rubber raft out from the side of this cliff. Or maybe they'll have a motor on it."

"A raft?" Dave said. "How do they get through a rock wall?"

"I guess what happened was, when the dam was put in, the pressure of the water backing up must have burst through the rock into a lower tunnel of the mine. It would have hollowed out kind of a cave. During the spring and summer, when the dam's full, the cave would be underwater. But this time of year, after the summer drought, the lake drops down to the cave level and they can run a boat or raft back in there."

Pap said, "I kind of remember that blowout now. I think there was even something in the paper about it." He blew a stream of smoke out into the cold night air. Tully shuddered. For a moment, a cigarette seemed almost appealing. Pap was a bad influence.

"They probably got a dock and everything back in that cave," Dave said. "Pretty slick."

"It is," Tully said. "I suspect they have the dock right below the shaft that goes to the lower level. Then all they have to do is winch the bales of marijuana down to the dock and load them onto a boat or raft."

Pap said, "This probably explains the scuba gear at the hotel, too. When the water's too high for a boat or raft, a couple of fellas in scuba outfits can drag the bales out underwater."

"Sounds about right to me," Tully said.

He motioned for silence. There had been an increase in watery sounds coming up from below. The three men leaned forward so that they could see better over the rock edge.

Then, as if by magic, a large rubber raft suddenly emerged from the side of the cliff. Tully hit it with a beam from the spotlight. Three men were in the raft, two in front paddling and one in back. The one in back held a weapon of some kind.

Tully handed the bullhorn to Pap.

"Pap Tully speaking." His voice boomed up and down the canyon. "The first quick move you fellas make will be your last. You there in the back, very slow and careful, lay that weapon in the bottom of the raft."

The man swung his weapon up toward the sound of Pap's voice.

Lem Scragg yelled from the front of the raft, "Throw down that gun, you fool, or he'll kill us all!"

The man with the weapon threw it to the floor of the raft.

"Shucks," Pap said. "It's a terrible thing when a man gets such a reputation."

"I know how disappointed you are," Tully said, taking back the bullhorn.

"Okay, now," he boomed through it, "I want you fellows to paddle up to where the road cuts down to the reservoir. And don't even accidentally touch a gun with so much as your toe, because you won't hear the shot that kills you."

The men started paddling.

"You okay, Pap?" Tully asked.

"I'm great, Bo. If this is still my birthday party, it's the best I ever had!"

"I'm glad. Consider it a thoughtful gift. As opposed to an expensive one. Now, can you walk along the road and keep these guys covered?"

"You bet."

"In that case, Dave and I will go get some vehicles and meet you down there."

Two Idaho State Police cruisers followed them down the road to the water. The ISP guys took the men out of the raft and cuffed them. As Tully expected, two of the men were the same two he had met at Littlefield's ranch, Robert Mitchell and Harry Kincaid. The man who had swung the weapon up at them had been Kincaid.

The State Police loaded the Littlefield crew into their vehicles. Tully carefully collected two Uzis from the bottom of the raft. He was pretty sure both guns would contain the fingerprints of Mitchell and Kincaid. The guns would match the casings used in the killings at the car.

Tully handcuffed Lem and put him in the back of his Explorer. He drove back to the parking lot at the new tunnel entrance. His deputies had all the workers out of the mine and standing in the parking lot. Some of the women were still crying. Tully felt sorry for them.

Ernie Thorpe walked over to the Explorer. "They all had ID of some kind, Bo. You count a library card as ID, don't you?"

"It's one of the best, Ernie. Load them all onto the bus and take them to their homes. We don't have room in the jail for practically a whole town. I doubt they'll be running off."

Ernie told the group they were going back to their homes in Famine. Some of the women stopped crying, but otherwise the announcement didn't provoke any outburst of joy. That's the problem with arresting folks who live in Famine, Tully thought.

Ernie brought Lister over and put him in the back seat of Tully's Explorer with Lem. One of the medics had bandaged up the rock cuts on his head. The top of his shirt was dark with blood and he still seemed a bit dazed.

Tully told Herb to escort the man in the earflap cap back to jail. "I'll talk to him in the morning."

He drove down the Last Hope Mine Road to the spot the berm had once occupied. Tully parked the car in nearly the same place where the Jeep Grand Cherokee had been shot up.

"Here's the way I think the shooting went down," Tully said. "I figure you and Lister were the shooters. One of you stood over there and the other one stood there. The Jeep comes up and stops at the berm. You spray automatic fire into the front seat, Lem."

"Close, but not close enough," Lem said.

"Lister has to wait," Tully went on, "because the guy who is setting them up is sitting on the right in the back seat. This guy opens the door and rolls out of the car. Lister then blasts the back seat. But because Lister hesitated, the guy in the left back seat, Holt, manages to get out. He's shooting wildly and manages to hit someone standing back in the woods. Holt then takes off running and is tracked down and shot by either you or Lister."

Lister shook his head, very gently, as if he had a terrible headache. Lem laughed.

"That is a remarkable piece of crime deduction," Lem said. "Basically, you got it right. But there are a couple of things wrong with it. First of all, Lister and me weren't the shooters."

"Easy for you to say," Tully said.

"I ain't going down for no murders," Lister whined.

"We were home that night," Lem went on. "But we knew all about the setup, okay? If we'd tried to stop it, they would have shot us. Not that we had any such foolish intention. Right, Lister?"

"Right."

"All you got to do is check the fingerprints on the Uzis in the boat," Lem said. "The only prints you find on them will be those of the guys that used them, Mitchell and Kincaid. They wouldn't let anybody else touch those guns, not even Lucas. The bullets in the bodies will match up with the Uzis."

Lem was almost cordial, giving the impression his whole purpose in life was to ingratiate himself with the sheriff. Thank goodness for sociopaths, Tully thought.

"Lucas?" he said. "You mean the guy in the earflap cap who sometimes works at the gas station for Ed Grange?"

"I don't know if 'work' is the right word. But Lucas Kincaid is one mean guy. Even Bob and Harry are scared of him."

"Lucas Kincaid?"

"Yeah, he's Harry's old man. He's a terrific tracker."

"He's the guy who tracked down Holt and killed him?" Tully said.

"He's the one. He did a lot of trapping, shooting coyotes for their pelts, that sort of stuff, until Grange started paying him a lot better money."

"So Mitchell and Harry Kincaid handle the marketing?"

"Mitchell does, anyway. I think Harry mostly kills people."

"So who shot Buck?"

"Lucas Kincaid. Shot him with his coyote gun. I think it's a two-twenty-three. The guy you found dead over Dad's fence emptied his gun and then threw it away. Lucas found it. It's a nice pearl-handled forty-five."

"We've already got it and the coyote gun. So who was the guy standing back in the woods?"

"Guess," said Lem.

"Vern Littlefield," Tully said.

"You got it! I don't think anybody knew he was

standing back in there. He apparently snuck out to see for himself how this thing was going to go down. They found him after the shooting."

"What did you do with the body?"

"We, me and Lister, didn't do anything with the body. We weren't there. I think Harry and his dad hauled it away. But there are a lot of prospect holes around. Be tough to find the one they dropped Vern into. And a whole lot tougher to get him out."

"Littlefield's vehicle would have still been at the mine," Tully said.

"Yeah, Mitchell called me early the next morning and said I'd probably find Vern's truck parked up there. He told me to drive it up to Vern's hunting camp and leave it there. Lister picked me up at the camp."

"The idea, I suppose, was everyone would think Vern got himself lost in the mountains hunting elk?" Tully said.

"Right."

"So your footprints will match the casts my CSI unit made of the tracks going up the mine road?"

"Yeah. Hey, what do you mean, CSI unit? You have a CSI unit?"

"One of the best," Tully said. "So who was the guy in the right rear seat who set all this up?"

"You're not going to believe this," Lem said.

"Ed Grange," Tully said. "Ed of Ed's Gas-N-Grub."

"You're right! How did you guess that?"

"Just lucky," Tully said. "Got him in jail already."

"Yeah, Ed ran the whole local operation. Littlefield put up the money, Bob and Harry flew the weed south.

You think the judge will go easy on me and Lister if we testify against them?"

"You never can tell. You and Lister aren't exactly the best witnesses in the world."

"Who else you got?"

"Good point. Okay, a couple more questions, Lem. Lucas Kincaid shot Buck, right?"

"Yeah, it was Lucas. You check out his rifles, you'll find the one used on Buck."

"I know. But who gave the order, Ed Grange?"

"I don't think Ed orders Lucas around, but he probably told him it would be a good idea for him to kill you. I imagine Kincaid took it from there."

"Did Lucas think he was shooting at me?" Tully asked.

"Yeah, Ed was mighty upset when he found out Lucas had hit Buck instead. He likes Buck. Anyway, I guess you gave Ed the impression you had this whole mess pretty well figured out."

Tully tugged on the corner of his mustache. "Yeah, I must have let that slip out. We won't have much trouble proving it was Littlefield killed back in the woods. The DNA from the pool of blood in the woods will match the DNA on the hairs from Vern's hairbrush. Apparently Lucas doesn't watch much TV. Otherwise, he'd know about shell casings and that the ejection and firing-pin marks on them are as individual as fingerprints."

"He probably doesn't even have a TV set," Lem said. "He lives so far back in the woods the sun don't shine there. But you sure don't want him on your trail."

"How about Cindy Littlefield? Was she in on this little caper?"

"Naw. She found out what was going on and apparently didn't like it. Mitchell was afraid the ranch hands might stumble on to something, too, and blab about it. So he fired them. But he couldn't fire Cindy. That's why Dana Cassidy was brought in from L.A., to keep an eye on her. Even before that, they hardly ever left her alone. If Mitchell went somewhere, he took her with him. I figure she had a date with a prospect hole herself."

"No doubt. By the way, Lem, what were you doing that night at the hotel?"

"What hotel?"

"Littlefield's old hotel on his ranch. The night after the killings."

"I've never been in that old hotel. For one thing, I hear it's haunted."

"Haunted!" cried Lister. "Nobody ever told me that!"

"A really stupid person may have been poking around there," Lem said. "But I have no idea who it might have been."

"I ain't stupid!" Lister said.

"I rest my case," Lem said.

"So, Lister, exactly what was your reason for being in the hotel?"

"Wasn't nothing, really. I just wanted to have a look at the pearl-handled forty-five that Holt fellow dropped. I was curious about it is all. Didn't plan on stealing it or anything. But the door was locked."

"Good thing you were just curious. Otherwise, you might be facing a murder rap for killing Littlefield."

"You think I didn't know that? But listen, the guy you should be arresting is the pervert hanging out in that hotel!"

"Pervert?" Pap said.

"Forget it," Tully said. "Now, Lem, here's the Sixty-Four-Thousand-Dollar Question. What was the reason Holt and the other two guys from L.A. were set up?"

"That's pretty obvious, don't you think? They were making so much money wholesaling and retailing the weed in L.A., they figured they could make a whole lot more if they cut themselves into the production side, too. You got to admit, the dam and the mine were a pretty sweet combination. Who would ever have figured that?"

Tully turned and gave Lem his biggest grin.

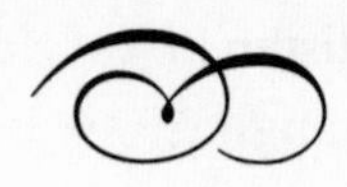

Chapter 51

It was early morning by the time Tully got back to Blight City. After booking Lem and Lister into the county jail, Tully drove Pap back to his mansion on the hill. Pap was sound asleep in the front seat, his head resting against the window.

"Wake up, Pap," Tully said, nudging the old man. "You're home."

Pap rubbed his eyes and looked around. "You mean my birthday party is finally over?"

"Yeah, it's over," Tully said. "To tell you the truth, I thought it might never end."

"Me, too."

Tully walked around and got the old man's pack out of the back of the Explorer. When he got to the little white gate, Pap still hadn't emerged from the vehicle. Tully walked back and opened the door.

"This blasted seat belt!" Pap snarled.

Tully reached across him and unlocked the belt. Old people, he thought.

Tully handed him the pack, and they went up the walk to the house. "I got to tell you, Pap, that was a pretty clever thing you did, shooting into the rock wall behind Lister."

"Wasn't so clever," Pap said. "I was aiming for the varmint's head."

Tully laughed. "I thought you might have. I just didn't expect you to admit it. Give me your key and I'll unlock your door."

It was Pap's turn to laugh. "When you got my reputation, Bo, you don't need to lock your doors."

"I expect that's true."

"On the other hand, you better knock."

"How come?"

"I got myself a live-in housekeeper, that's how come."

Tully knocked on the door. "I don't know if I can stand too many more surprises."

A young woman opened the door. She had a bathrobe pulled tightly around her. Pap slid in past her and headed for the bathroom. He dropped his pack in the middle of the hallway.

"Pap!" the housekeeper shouted. "You know that doesn't go there! Put it where it belongs!"

Sheepishly, Pap scurried back, picked up the pack and carried it off with him.

"Deedee!" Tully said.

"Yeah, Sheriff, I'm your dad's new housekeeper. What do you think of that?"

"I'm flabbergasted!"

"A lot of people are. But I needed a new job, and Pap needed a housekeeper. So there you go."

"He's an awfully ornery old guy."

"That's only his reputation. He's really an old softy."

"I'll bet he's that, all right."

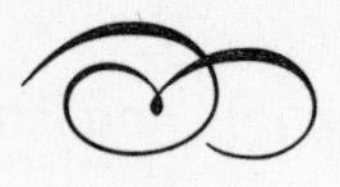

Chapter 52

Tully stopped by the office before heading home. The briefing room was full of both the night shift and the day shift deputies. They stood and broke into applause when Tully walked in. He smiled and thanked them. He tried the coffee thermoses. Empty. He looked at the doughnut tray. Empty. The deputies trooped out around him, some of them giving him a pat on the shoulder. They were a good bunch.

Daisy was standing there looking tired and solemn. Herb gave him a little wave and then went back into his cubicle. Ernie Thorpe was standing by Tully's office door, beaming.

"Why the sad face, Daisy?" Tully said, walking past her.

"Don't ask," she said.

"You do good work, Thorpe!" he said to the deputy.

"Thanks. But even better than that, Sheriff, I think I may have saved your life."

"How's that?

"Well, I glanced into your office just as a Hobo spider almost as big as my hand rushed out from behind your filing cabinet. Man, did I ever whomp that sucker. Them Hobos can kill you, Sheriff, you know that?"

Tully stared at him.

"Go home, Thorpe," he said.

He walked into his office and slumped into his chair.

He picked up the phone and dialed. A male voice answered. "Yup."

"Batim?"

"Yup.

"It's Sheriff Bo Tully, Batim."

"Well, Bo. How you doing?"

"I'm doing fine, Batim. How about you?"

"I'm doing great."

"I just called to tell you I'm sorry about the boys."

"Hey, Bo, don't even think about it. I can use the rest."

"I don't expect we'll have any murder charges against them, once we get everything sorted out. They'll probably be away for a couple years, though."

"Sounds wonderful."

"I suppose you heard about Vern Littlefield."

"Yeah, that's a real pity. Vern and I never got along too good, what with his cattle constantly jumping over my fences and all, but I'll miss him."

"One thing I want to know, Batim. What were you doing over at the murder scene?"

"How'd you know?"

"A matchstick you'd been chewing on. I don't want to go to all the expense of checking your DNA on it, so tell me right now what you were doing there."

"The fact is, Bo, I just got curiouser and curiouser about the whole situation and finally had to go over there and check it out for myself. It was a nasty piece of work."

"Okay, that's good enough for me. We'll forget about the match."

"Tell me, Bo, was the widow Littlefield involved?"

"Not according to Lem and Lister. I'm going to release her today and have somebody drive her home. You interested in her, Batim?"

"That's a mighty big ranch for a little lady like her to run. Maybe she'll need some help."

"You never can tell. Of course, you'd probably have to take a bath at least once a week."

"Hey, Bo, I clean up pretty good, when there's a reason to."

When he was done talking to Batim, Tully called Susan.

"You want to go camping?" he asked.

"In October?"

"Yeah," Tully said. He looked out the window. Principal Jan Whittle's car had just pulled in next to his. That rotten brat of a Cliff kid had run off again!

"Actually," he told Susan, "it might be November. Looks as if I may have to snowshoe over a couple mountain ranges first."

"November," Susan said. "Well, that's more like it. I'd love to go camping with you in November."

"I'll bring a tent heater," he said.

"Probably won't need one," she said.

About the Author

Patrick McManus is a renowned outdoor writer, humorist and long-time columnist for *Outdoor Life* and *Field and Stream*. He is the author of many books, including such runaway *New York Times* bestsellers as *The Grasshopper Trap, The Night the Bear Ate Goombaw* and *Real Ponies Don't Go Oink!* He lives in Spokane, Washington.